AGAINST THE ODDS

For a moment Elizabeth couldn't move. If she screamed, no one would hear her. If she went inside to try to save Ronnie, Max would take her captive.

I've got to call the police! she realized. As she backed away from the window, she looked around for a phone booth. There wasn't one in sight. Elizabeth ran around to the back of the building, wincing as her feet noisily hit the gravel.

She found an abandoned gas station on the other side of the building, and there, on the wall, was an old, rusty phone booth.

Elizabeth sprinted up to it and picked up the receiver. Her heart jumped when she heard a faint dial tone. She struggled to keep her fingers steady as she dialed 911.

"Emergency," a voice at the other end answered.

"Hello, I'm—"

But those were the only words she could get out before a large hand clamped over her mouth.

"Aughh—"

A choked scream was all Elizabeth could manage as she felt herself being dragged backward toward the building.

Bantam Books in the Sweet Valley High Series
Ask your bookseller for the books you have missed

SWEET VALLEY HIGH

AGAINST THE ODDS

Written by
Kate William

Created by
FRANCINE PASCAL

BANTAM BOOKS
TORONTO • NEW YORK • LONDON • SYDNEY • AUCKLAND

RL 6, IL age 12 and up

AGAINST THE ODDS
A Bantam Book / January 1989

Sweet Valley High is a registered trademark of Francine Pascal.

Conceived by Francine Pascal.

*Produced by Daniel Weiss Associates, Inc.,
27 West 20th Street, New York, NY 10011*

Cover art by James Mathewuse

ISBN 0-553-27650-6

Published simultaneously in the United States and Canada

*Bantam Books are published by Bantam Books, a division of Bantam Doubleday
Dell Publishing Group, Inc. Its trademark, consisting of the words "Bantam
Books" and the portrayal of a rooster, is Registered in U.S. Patent and Trademark
Office and in other countries. Marca Registrada. Bantam Books, 666 Fifth Avenue,
New York, New York 10103.*

PRINTED IN THE UNITED STATES OF AMERICA

O   0 9 8 7 6 5 4 3 2 1

*With thanks to
GHC,
soccer legend.*

One

Elizabeth Wakefield shot a quick glance at the scoreboard. There were only forty-five seconds remaining in the game, and the Sweet Valley Gladiators were tied with the Palisades Pumas.

"I *hate* time-outs," Enid Rollins, Elizabeth's best friend, said. "They always happen just when the game is getting exciting!"

Elizabeth nodded in agreement. The tension was almost too much to bear. If the Gladiators lost this game, they would be eliminated from the championships. If they won, they would end the season in a tie with Big Mesa for first place in their division. The two teams would have to face each other the next Saturday in a special play-off game.

If it were any other Sweet Valley team, the outcome of the game wouldn't have meant quite so much to Elizabeth. But her boyfriend, Jeffrey

French, was on the soccer team, and that meant all the difference in the world.

Elizabeth smiled as she thought about Jeffrey. For days he had been so excited about the game that he could barely talk about anything else. But Elizabeth hadn't really minded. In fact, she admired his winning attitude. It was almost as if he were incapable of giving less than one hundred percent. Jeffrey wasn't one of the team's highest scorers or flashiest players—his best friend, Aaron Dallas, fit those descriptions. But in his own dependable, enthusiastic way, Jeffrey was the backbone of the team, and Elizabeth knew that Jeffrey was one of the main reasons the Gladiators had done so well that year.

"Let's go, Gladiators!" the cheerleaders yelled. Elizabeth looked down to see her twin sister, Jessica, waving her pom-poms energetically, leading the cheer. Immediately Jessica caught Elizabeth's glance, and her face broke into a wide grin. "He's going to do it—you—wait!" Jessica shouted. Then she looked slightly to Elizabeth's right and blew a kiss to her boyfriend, A. J. Morgan. A few students in front turned around to see who the kiss was headed for, and A.J. blushed.

Elizabeth laughed. *Leave it to Jessica to steal the attention away from the most exciting game of the year*, she thought.

Even after sixteen years, Elizabeth was still amazed by the differences between herself and Jessica. On the surface they were mirror images—Elizabeth's eyes shone with the same sparkling blue-green as Jessica's, and her hair was the identical shade of blond. Her perfect size-six figure, the dimple in her left cheek, even the gold lavaliere she wore around her neck—everything matched Jessica exactly.

But for all their similarities in looks, their personalities couldn't have been more different. For every conservatively stylish outfit Elizabeth had, Jessica had one that was wild and trendy. Elizabeth enjoyed long walks with Jeffrey and deep talks late into the night with Enid. Her greatest dream was to become a writer, and she loved working for *The Oracle*, Sweet Valley High's newspaper. But to Jessica long talks were fine only if *she* was the topic of conversation. And she had no patience for sticking to one thing: *her* interests changed from week to week, depending on what project excited her the most at the moment. The latest project was creating earrings that Jessica was convinced would revolutionize the jewelry world.

Of course, there *were* times that Jessica had tried to change—for instance, when she had first met A.J. She had thought he only liked conservative and studious girls, so she tried to behave like one. As usual with Jessica, she had gone overboard, becoming so quiet that A.J. had gotten bored with her. Fortunately she had come to her senses before it was too late, and she and A.J. were now closer than ever.

A sudden roar from the crowd made Elizabeth snap out of her thoughts, and she quickly located the action on the center of the field. A pack of players from both teams had converged on the ball. Suddenly a tall, blond figure emerged. As he ran down the field, his tousled hair blew out behind him in the breeze.

"Yea, Jeffrey!" Elizabeth cried at the top of her lungs.

Enid let out a loud whistle. "Go for it!" she yelled, grabbing Elizabeth's hand and squeezing it. Her curly brown hair bounced up and down as she jumped with excitement. On Elizabeth's left, Julie Porter clapped her hands and cheered.

"Ten seconds remaining!" the announcer's voice bellowed over the PA system.

Jeffrey continued to maneuver skillfully toward the Puma goal, past three more defenders. He faked left and went right, causing the goalie to lean the wrong way. Then, with lightning-quick reflexes, Jeffrey drew his foot back and kicked the ball directly toward the goal.

The goalie scrambled to recover his balance, but the ball flew past him into the back of the net.

"Score!" the announcer yelled.

A thunderous roar erupted in the Sweet Valley bleachers. Enid and Julie both threw their arms around Elizabeth.

"It was all because of Liz," Enid said. "Seriously! Did you notice Jeffrey looking at you just before he scored?"

Elizabeth giggled. "Sure, Enid," she said. "And didn't you hear him call out my name just as he kicked the ball?"

"Well," Enid said with a shrug, "at least that's the way *I* saw it."

At the sound of the final buzzer, the entire Sweet Valley team swarmed around Jeffrey on the field. As they lifted him up high onto their shoulders, he threw back his head and laughed.

"Come on," Enid urged, starting to climb down the bleachers. "Don't you want to congratulate him?"

"Sure I do. I'll be right there," Elizabeth said. But for a moment she wanted to stand still and take it all in. Jeffrey looked so wonderful, and she wanted to remember this moment for a long time.

Loud music, laughter, and conversation greeted Elizabeth and Jeffrey as they walked arm in arm into the Dairi Burger, followed by Enid and her boyfriend, Hugh Grayson. Elizabeth had never seen the place so crowded before; it was a real celebration.

"Get ready for a hero's welcome," Enid warned Jeffrey.

He laughed. "Oh, come on, Enid. I wasn't the only—"

"Hey, there's the man of the hour!" Aaron Dallas's voice rang out above the din.

Jeffrey's face turned pink as people yelled out his name in congratulations.

In the center of the crowd, some of Jeffrey's teammates were shouting the loudest: Aaron, Tony Esteban, Michael Schmidt, and Brad Tomasi. Flashing a wide grin, Aaron broke away from them and squeezed through the crowd to Elizabeth and Jeffrey. "Enjoy it, buddy," he said. "A little hero worship never hurt anyone!"

"I don't know about that," Jeffrey said wryly. "Look at what it did to you!"

Aaron laughed and punched him playfully in the shoulder. "Watch it, French!"

Elizabeth smiled. She remembered a time when Jeffrey couldn't have kidded around with Aaron, back when Aaron was angry about his parents' divorce. But with Jeffrey's help, Aaron had managed to pull through the hard times, and once again they were the best of friends.

Elizabeth felt a tug on her sleeve. "Come on, Liz. I can't save these seats forever, you know!"

Jessica was pointing to a long table in the

back. Chatting away on either side of A.J., with their shoulder bags and jackets thrown over four empty seats, were Lila Fowler and Amy Sutton. Even though Elizabeth found both girls snobby, they were two of Jessica's best friends, and she had learned to get along with them—most of the time. Smiling politely, she led Jeffrey, Enid, and Hugh to the table.

"How does it feel to be the star of the team, Jeffrey?" Jessica asked as Lila and Amy cleared the seats around the table.

"Well, I don't know about that," Jeffrey said with an embarrassed chuckle. "I mean, I could still screw up in next week's game."

Jessica groaned. "Jeffrey, you're too modest. I'm afraid my sister is rubbing off on you."

"Hey, just a minute!" Elizabeth protested.

With a giggle, Jessica squeezed around the table toward her chair, which was wedged tightly against the wall. As she leaned over the table to balance herself before she slid into it, one of her earrings flew off, landing with a clatter on the table.

"Uh, tell me something," Enid said, lifting the large earring made of black plastic and dangling, sparkling beads. "Is this a Christmas tree ornament or an earring?"

Everyone at the table burst out laughing—except for Jessica. Raising an eyebrow, she took the earring from Enid and put it back on.

"For your information, these happen to be *the* latest fashion."

Enid shrugged. "I have to admit, I've never seen anything like them."

"That's because Jessica made them herself," Lila Fowler said, sounding proud of her friend. Lila was known as the richest, snobbiest girl in Sweet Valley, but she had her loyalties—and Jessica was one of them.

"Just wait till she starts marketing them," Amy Sutton added, giving Enid a triumphant look. "*Then* we'll see who's laughing."

Elizabeth looked up to see Ronnie Edwards sauntering up to the table, dressed in an expensive-looking designer shirt and pleated pants. It was a far cry from his usual jeans and rugby shirt, she noted.

"Hey, look who's here!" a voice suddenly called out. "I guess this is the table of honor," Ronnie commented. "What'll you guys have? I'm taking orders—it's on me!"

"Uh-oh," Enid muttered under her breath.

An uneasy silence fell over the table. Elizabeth remembered all too well that Ronnie had once been Enid's boyfriend—and she could never forget the rotten way he had treated Enid after becoming insanely jealous over an innocent letter she had received from a former boyfriend.

Ronnie stood by the table, his sapphire-blue eyes twinkling. "Come on, don't be shy! Get whatever you want. You guys deserve nothing but the best!"

Elizabeth gave Jeffrey an uncertain look.

He smiled at Ronnie. "Uh, that's really nice of you," he said, "but we're all set. Besides, there are a lot of people at the table—"

"Hey, money is no object," Ronnie insisted. With a flourish, he pulled a wad of bills out of his pocket. "I got a good deal on my Mustang convertible, and somehow I had all this left over, too. Not bad, huh?"

Elizabeth noticed three surly-looking guys at the counter who were staring intently at Ronnie's money. They looked too old to be high-school students, and with their sunglasses, beard stubble, and leather jackets they seemed like the kind of guys it would be better to stay away from. Elizabeth hoped that Ronnie would quiet down and put his money away before they got too interested.

"Well, look who won the lottery," Lila said with a smirk.

"Better than that," Ronnie said. "I earned it."

"Oh, please," Lila said with a dismissive wave of her hand. "What have you been doing, mowing every lawn in Sweet Valley since the age of two?"

Ronnie smiled. "No, let's just say I've got connections."

9

"I get it," Amy said dryly. "One of your friends robbed a bank, right?"

"No, nothing like that," Ronnie said, chuckling.

Lila raised her eyebrows knowingly. "Well, then, it has to be some kind of inheritance or trust fund or something."

"I wish," Ronnie replied. "Anyway, that's not impor—"

"Come on," Jessica pleaded, her curiosity piqued. "How *did* you get it?"

Elizabeth saw a look of disgust cross Jeffrey's face. Abruptly he stood up from the table and said, "I'm really thirsty. I think I'll go get a round of sodas for the table."

Puzzled, Elizabeth watched Jeffrey walk toward the counter. Within seconds he was surrounded by students congratulating him about the game.

Looking over his shoulder at Jeffrey, Ronnie shrugged. "I hope I didn't offend anyone. I only wanted to—"

He was cut off by a gravelly voice. "Yo, did I hear you say you had a Mustang convertible?" One of the three guys from the counter was standing next to Ronnie, a cigarette dangling from his mouth.

"Yeah," Ronnie said uneasily.

"No kidding," he said. "Great car, man! I haven't seen the new model yet. Is that the one you have?"

"Yep. It's pretty incredible, too. You wouldn't believe the acceleration. . . ."

Elizabeth stopped listening to their conversation, along with everyone else at the table. "This is too weird," Enid muttered to Elizabeth. She stood up and walked off to the counter, followed by Hugh.

"Well, leave it to Ronnie to really bring this table to life," Amy said.

"So anyway," Jessica continued, as if nothing had happened, "I'm not sure I want to start marketing my jewelry right away. I think it's important to develop a small local reputation first, don't you think?"

"Uh, listen, guys," Ronnie interrupted. "We're going to go outside for a second to look at my car, but I'll be right back. Remember what I said: I expect this table to be full of food and drinks the next time I see it!"

Deep in conversation about jewelry, Jessica and her friends ignored Ronnie. But Elizabeth kept her eye on him as he walked outside. It was weird, the way that guy had just come up and talked to Ronnie. They didn't even know each other.

She glanced quickly around the room. Jeffrey was deep in the crowd, still inching his way to the counter. Off to his left, the other two tough-looking guys were staring at the front door. They seemed to be waiting for something or someone.

Then, as if on cue, one of the guys looked at his watch. Liz could see his lips form the word *now*. When the two men straightened up, they bolted out the front door after Ronnie and their friend.

Elizabeth stood up and tried to push her way through the crowd toward Jeffrey. She had a feeling Ronnie was in trouble.

Two

"I don't know how you scored that goal, French!" said Brad Tomasi, the Gladiators' left wing.

Michael Schmidt, the team's co-captain with Aaron, shook his head. "It was pretty amazing. There were three guys covering you on the play!"

"No, there weren't, Mike," Jeffrey protested. Then an impish grin spread across his face. "There were four."

As his teammates broke up laughing, Jeffrey caught sight of Elizabeth squeezing her way through the crowd toward him. He smiled, but then he saw that her face was lined with concern.

"Liz, are you all right?"

Elizabeth grabbed Jeffrey's hand. "I'm fine. But I need to talk to you for a second."

"Be right back," Jeffrey told his friends. As he followed Elizabeth toward the door, he chuckled. "What's up? Are there reporters waiting for me outside?"

"It's Ronnie," Elizabeth said in a serious tone. "I think he's in trouble."

"Oh, yeah? Did he run out of cash or something?"

"No, but he might soon. There were these really creepy-looking guys standing at the counter, Jeffrey. I could see them watching Ronnie when he was flashing all that money around. Anyway, one of them came up to the table and started talking to Ronnie about his car. Then they walked outside, and the guy's friends followed a couple of minutes later, as if they had timed it."

Jeffrey frowned. "Where did they go?"

"I guess out to the parking lot. I mean, maybe I'm overreacting. Maybe they really do just want to look at the car, but—"

"I'll be right back," Jeffrey said without waiting for her to finish.

"This way." Ronnie pointed. "It's on the other side of the parking lot."

"I want to show you my Lamborghini first," answered the guy in the leather jacket, who had introduced himself as Bruno. "I keep it hidden in the back, so no one paws all over it. People can be weird about nice cars."

14

"Right," Ronnie said with a laugh. "I know what you mean."

Ronnie smiled as he followed Bruno to the back of the Dairi Burger. For months he had been driving around in the old Toyota his mother had left behind after his parents' divorce. Who'd ever have thought he'd ever drive a car nice enough to think about hiding? *Thank you, Big Al,* he thought.

Even though he had never met Al Remsen, Ronnie felt as if the man had changed his life. Things hadn't been going too well between Ronnie and his father lately, and money had been tight. Ronnie had heard of Big Al through a customer at his father's all-night grocery store. At first he had been reluctant to deal with a bookie, especially Big Al, who had a reputation as the coldest, toughest guy in the business. But he was also the richest, and the whole thing had turned out to be so easy. All Ronnie had to do was put down a few dollars on high-school teams from Al's sheet, which listed the odds on all the area games. Ronnie seemed to have a knack for betting, and each week his winnings grew. Soon Al had become like an uncle to him, letting him bet on credit, lending him the car . . .

Ronnie laughed to himself over his white lie about the Mustang. He knew it wouldn't hurt anyone to think he actually owned it.

15

A minute later Ronnie and Bruno reached the back wall of the Dairi Burger. There, a high wooden fence formed a dark alleyway behind the building.

Ronnie peered around the corner. Aside from an overflowing Dumpster, the spot seemed to be empty. The eerie hum of an air conditioner was the only sound that broke the silence. Ronnie felt a sudden twinge of fear.

"Uh, what's going on, Bruno?" he asked.

"What do you think?" an unfamiliar voice demanded.

Ronnie whirled around to see two shadowy figures entering the alley. One of them, a heavyset guy with dark beard stubble, just folded his arms across his large chest and glared back at Ronnie. The other, who had blond hair and wore a ripped leather jacket, approached Ronnie and leered. "Now, Mr. Big Spender, why don't you share a little of that pocket money with your friends?"

The setting sun cast a long shadow in front of Jeffrey as he ran around to the back of the Dairi Burger. As he got closer, he heard scuffling noises, and then a quivering voice saying, "All right, all right. J-just leave me alone for a second." Then he heard a scream.

He sprinted around the corner into the alleyway. There, in the shadows, he saw three figures clustered around another person who was backing toward the Dumpster. As his eyes adjusted to the darkness, Jeffrey could tell the one in trouble was Ronnie.

One of the guys was pushing Ronnie up against the Dumpster. "I didn't like that scream, buddy," he said. "It hurt my ears. I think we're going to raise our cash request a few hundred bucks to cover ear doctor expenses."

"Easy, Bruno," Ronnie said, his hand fumbling in his pocket. "Give me a chance."

"Hey, check it out," one of the other guys said. Bruno, Ronnie, and the other guy spun around to see Jeffrey walking steadily toward them.

Jeffrey fixed his gaze on each of their faces as he spoke. "Doesn't seem like you guys are playing fair, does it?" he said. "I mean, three against one doesn't exactly seem like a good match in my book."

"Who's this dude?" the dark-haired guy asked.

"He—he's the star of the soccer team!" Ronnie blurted.

Bruno looked at Jeffrey with disdain. "Well, *star*," he said, "I think you're in the wrong place. You wouldn't score too many goals with a crushed foot. Right, guys?"

As the other two grunted their approval, Jeffrey shook his head and laughed. "I'm really worried," he said. His eyes didn't waver an inch from Bruno's as he walked closer. "Listen, tough guy, if you want to take him on, you're going to have to include me in the fun."

Jeffrey's six-foot frame loomed over Bruno, who took a tentative step backward. "You're asking for trouble, pal," Bruno replied. "How do I know you're so tough?"

Jeffrey's hand suddenly shot up and grabbed the collar of Bruno's leather jacket. "Try me," he said through gritted teeth.

Out of the corner of his eye, Jeffrey could see Bruno's friends moving away toward the parking lot.

"Hey, hey, take it easy," Bruno said, a note of defensiveness creeping into his voice. His eyes were wide with bewilderment as he looked over Jeffrey's shoulder. "Hey, where are you guys going? We've got some business to take care of!"

"Nothing doing, man," the blond guy said. "We're out of here."

Bruno swallowed as his friends took off. Forcing a smile, he said, "We were only fooling around. We weren't really going to take anything."

"Right," Jeffrey said. "You just like to harass people in alleyways for fun. I get it." He released Bruno's collar. "Well, looks to me like your pals don't want to play anymore. I think if you want to catch up to them, you're going to have to run."

"Uh, yeah," Bruno said, adjusting his jacket. "See you around." With his chin held high, Bruno turned and walked out of the alley. But as soon as he disappeared around the corner of the building, Jeffrey could hear his footsteps breaking into a run.

Jeffrey turned to Ronnie, who was staring at him with awe. "Are you OK?" he asked.

"That was incredible!" Ronnie said. He stepped forward and shook Jeffrey's hand vigorously. "Thanks! I mean, those guys would have killed me if it weren't for you. I don't know how you did it!"

Jeffrey smiled. "Just a little tough talk, that's all. I could tell those guys would back off. I've seen the type before—all talk, no guts."

"You don't understand." Ronnie looked down and took a deep breath. "I've never told anyone this, but my whole life I've never been able to fight. When somebody threatens me, I'm a basket case. People think I'm so tough, but I can't even talk tough, let alone hurt anyone!" Suddenly he reached into his pocket. "Here, let me repay you."

Jeffrey put up his hand, signaling Ronnie to put his money away. The week before, he had seen Ronnie hanging out with a sinister-looking guy who sometimes lurked around the soccer field. Rumor had it the guy was a gambler, and after Ronnie's little display inside the Dairi Burger, Jeffrey had quickly put two and two together. Ronnie was making his fortune betting on Sweet Valley High games. There was no way he would accept any money Ronnie had made gambling. Just the thought of high-school gambling turned Jeffrey's stomach. If people could be hooked on it at this level, there was no telling what would happen to them later on.

"I insist," Ronnie said, thrusting a few twenty-dollar bills at Jeffrey. "I mean, you didn't have to help me out."

"I didn't do this for a reward," Jeffrey said, trying to be as good-natured as possible. "Save it for the bill you ran up inside."

Ronnie put the money back in his pocket. "You're an incredible guy, you know that? Someday I'm going to pay you back for this, I promise."

"Seriously, Ronnie, don't even try," Jeffrey answered, walking back to the parking lot.

Ronnie fell in step with Jeffrey and put his arm around Jeffrey's shoulder. "You know, Jeff, it's nice to meet someone who really cares about other people. I'll never forget what you did for me."

At first Jeffrey felt like shaking Ronnie's arm off and telling him to get lost, but he stopped himself. It was hard to be mean to someone who seemed to need friends so much. That was probably the reason Ronnie was showing off in the Dairi Burger. Jeffrey didn't know Ronnie that well, but he did know that people always seemed to be turned off by Ronnie's aggressive nature, and that made him work even harder to get people to like him. It was a vicious cycle—the more he tried, the more people disliked him. Now that Ronnie had a little money, he probably thought he could buy friendship.

Jeffrey had to admit that Ronnie wasn't really that bad as a person. He was just a little rough around the edges. Maybe if people were a little nicer to him, he wouldn't feel the need to gamble.

As the two of them walked back to the front of the Dairi Burger, Jeffrey slapped Ronnie on the back. "Come on," he said. "After what you've been through, I think you could use an ice-cream soda. *My* treat."

Three

Elizabeth twirled a french fry absentmindedly in her fingers as she looked up at the clock. It was a typical Monday at the Sweet Valley High cafeteria, with everyone talking excitedly about the past weekend. To her left, Jessica, A.J., Lila, and Amy were deep in conversation. Elizabeth usually didn't sit with them, but Enid was working on an art project, most of the *Oracle* editors were on assignment, and Jeffrey hadn't shown up yet. When A.J. had seen that Elizabeth was alone, he pulled up a seat for her.

This isn't like Jeffrey at all, Elizabeth said to herself. For what seemed like the hundredth time, she scanned the room to see if he had arrived.

"What happened to Jeffrey?" A.J. asked, having noticed her somber mood.

Elizabeth shrugged. "Who knows? Maybe he ad something to do with the team."

"In the middle of the day?" Lila asked, over-earing the conversation.

"Liz, don't worry," Jessica reassured her. "He's 1st a little late. Besides"—her face broke into a vide grin—"you have *our* scintillating company."

Elizabeth rolled her eyes. "Right," she said. How could I ever forget?"

Suddenly Jessica spotted something behind lizabeth. "Look!" she cried out.

"Is it Jeffrey?" Elizabeth said.

"No, it's my earrings!" Jessica waved across he cafeteria. "Hey, Cara!" she called. "Where lid you get those *fabulous* creations? London, New York, or Paris?"

Cara Walker, who had just returned her mpty tray to the conveyor belt, threw back her ong, dark hair and let out a laugh. She was vith Jean West and Sandra Bacon, two other heerleaders, who both smiled when they saw essica. "Right here in Sweet Valley! They're riginal Wakefields," Cara called back, finger-ng her earrings, "given to me personally by the lesigner. Her designs are really hot these days."

As the three girls walked toward them, Eliza-eth looked at the earrings. She wasn't crazy bout the design, but the small, bright-colored eathers did set off Cara's complexion nicely.

"Don't they look wonderful?" Jessica gushed o Elizabeth.

"They're really *unusual*, Jess," Elizabeth replied.

"Liz, you're just humoring me—I can tell!" Jessica said with a pout.

"No, really, I—"

"Well, you don't have to like them." Jessica turned back to Cara and her friends, who were pulling up chairs opposite her. "Other people do. Even A.J. likes them."

"Sure." A.J. nodded and took the last sip of his milk shake. But Elizabeth could tell by his tone of voice that he didn't really care that much for the earrings, one way or the other.

"Hey, guys," Cara said. "How does it feel to be in the presence of a future famous designer?"

"Who's that?" Elizabeth teased.

Jessica raised an eyebrow and glared at her sister. "Liz, you just don't recognize true talent sometimes. Maybe you haven't noticed, but for months and months I've been looking at all the designs—checking out what's new on the market, what people are buying. I didn't just throw some materials together, you know. This was a very scientific."

"I know, I know," Elizabeth said with a smile. "I was only teasing."

"Just wait until the lady at the Treasure Island boutique sees my stuff," Jessica said.

"You mean you actually called her?" Sandra asked.

"I sure did," Jessica answered. "Just before lunch. She told me to come by after school today. In fact, Lila and Amy and I were just talking about a plan. . . ."

Cara, Jean, Sandra, Lila, and Amy all leaned forward to listen to Jessica. Just then Elizabeth felt a gentle nudge in her ribs.

"There he is," A.J. said.

Elizabeth looked up to see Jeffrey walking into the cafeteria, with Ronnie right behind him. A guilty smile crept across Jeffrey's face as he hurried over to the table and sat down across from Elizabeth. "Sorry I'm so late," he said, quickly opening his lunch bag and unwrapping a sandwich.

"It's OK. You'd better hurry up and eat, though," Elizabeth said good-naturedly. "There're only a few minutes left."

"It's all my fault," Ronnie said, pulling up a chair next to Jeffrey. "I was talking his ear off about our social studies assignment."

"Mm-hmm," Elizabeth replied.

Her terse reaction wasn't lost on Ronnie. Looking a little uncomfortable, he said, "Well, I guess I'd better get some lunch."

Before he could stand up, Jessica said, "Wait a minute, Ronnie. We want your honest opinion." She pointed to Cara's earrings. "Would you buy these for your girlfriend?"

"My—my girlfriend?" Ronnie stuttered. Everyone knew Ronnie hadn't had a girlfriend in a long time.

"You know, if you wanted to give her something really nice and fashionable," Jessica continued. "Something out of the ordinary."

"Uh—sure!" Ronnie said, glancing quickly at the earrings. "They're nice. Must be pretty expensive."

Jessica turned to Elizabeth and grinned triumphantly. "You see, even guys can tell. I just *know* there's a big market for these." Then she sighed and slumped a bit in her seat. "It's too bad I won't be able to take advantage of it."

There was a puzzled silence. "What do you mean take advantage?" Ronnie finally asked.

"Well, it would take me *ages* to make enough money to buy the materials. I mean, it's incredible how much some of these beads and stones cost." She fingered her own earrings. "Not to mention the feathers and the tiny rubber tubes. Then you throw in the string, the clasps, the glue—and forget it if you want to use semi-precious stones."

Ronnie nodded distractedly. He cast an anxious glance toward the lunch line.

Elizabeth had a feeling she knew what her sister was going to say next. By now she was an expert at recognizing Jessica's I-need-something tone of voice.

"What I really need is some sort of financial

backer," Jessica said wistfully. "Someone with a sense of adventure who doesn't mind taking a risk with money."

Right again, Elizabeth said to herself. She could see Ronnie beginning to pay attention at the mention of the word *money*. Jessica had him right where she wanted him.

Lila snickered. "A risk with money, huh? That leaves out my father. He only likes guaranteed interest and stuff like that."

"Oh, well," Jessica replied with a shrug. "I guess this is just one of those once-in-a-lifetime opportunities that'll be wasted." She sighed.

"How much would you need, Jessica?" Ronnie asked.

Jessica shrugged as if to say the situation was so hopeless, she hadn't even bothered to add it all up. "Oh, I don't know. About five hundred dollars or so, I guess."

Ronnie laughed. "I thought you were talking about *big* money, like one or two grand!"

"Well," Jessica said, barely concealing the glee in her voice, "I could *really* do amazing things if I had that much." She gave Ronnie an innocent, quizzical look. "Why, do you know someone who might want to invest that much?"

Elizabeth could see A.J. getting a little agitated by Jessica's flirtatious tone of voice. "I'm sure you'll be able to find someone, Jess," he said.

"Probably," Ronnie agreed. "But if you don't, let me know. I think I'd be able to loan you a grand or so."

"What a generous offer, Ronnie," Jessica said with a radiant smile. "Maybe I'll take you up on it someday."

"Well, the offer will stand," Ronnie said, returning her smile. "I'd be glad to help out."

"Uh, if you want your lunch, I think you'd better go," A.J. interrupted, glaring at Ronnie.

Ronnie turned around. A cafeteria worker was just starting to put away some of the food. "Be right back," he said, getting up.

Immediately Jessica began chattering with her friends. After looking down at his watch, Jeffrey started to wolf down his lunch. Moments later Ronnie returned, full of questions for Jeffrey about social studies.

As both conversations continued on either side of her, Elizabeth began to feel more and more frustrated by the situation. She couldn't believe Jeffrey was choosing to spend his whole lunch period with Ronnie instead of her—and he didn't even like Ronnie. Almost no one did.

It wasn't until after the bell rang that Elizabeth had a chance to talk to Jeffrey alone. But as they walked down the hallway to class, she felt a little awkward with him.

"So, what do you think of Jessica's idea?" she said, trying to be cheerful.

"I don't know," Jeffrey answered. "Those earrings are really—"

"Weird?" Elizabeth suggested.

"Well . . ." Jeffrey looked over his shoulder to make sure Jessica and her friends weren't around. "Actually, *ugly* was more the word I was looking for."

Elizabeth giggled. She could feel her spirits slowly lifting. One look at his smiling green eyes was enough to make her forget she was angry.

Jeffrey looked relieved. "Good, a smile! You were mad at me, weren't you?"

Elizabeth hesitated, not sure what she should say about Ronnie. "I guess I'm frustrated more than anything else," she said after a moment, "I mean, Ronnie really monopolized you during lunch."

"I know," Jeffrey said. "Ever since I helped him out of that fight, he's been acting like I'm his best friend."

"Some best friend," Elizabeth murmured.

"Don't tell me," Jeffrey said, a mischievous glint in his eyes. "You've switched on me. You're Jessica, right? That didn't sound like the Elizabeth I know!"

Elizabeth couldn't help but crack a smile. "You know what I mean. Anyway, I'm biased. Ronnie was really rotten to Enid when they were going out—not to mention how he acted at the

Dairi Burger Saturday." She looked at him meaningfully. "Frankly, I can think of better people you could spend your time with."

"You know, you're right," Jeffrey said. With a warm look he put his arm around her waist and looked straight into her eyes. "It's just that I get tired of Aaron's jokes."

"Oooh!" Elizabeth said, pulling away from him. She let out a little scream as Jeffrey squeezed her tighter. "That's another reason you shouldn't spend so much time with Ronnie Edwards," she said with a giggle. "Your sense of humor's getting worse!"

As they walked down the hall, arm in arm, Elizabeth felt much happier. But she couldn't help feeling a little uneasy about Ronnie: his bragging at the Dairi Burger, the guys trying to mug him, the offer to back Jessica with a thousand dollars. . . . He had to be getting all that money *somewhere*, and Elizabeth had a feeling it wasn't from working at his father's grocery store.

No matter how hard she tried to convince herself otherwise, she was sure something strange was going on with Ronnie. And the fact that he was starting to latch onto Jeffrey only made things worse.

Four

"So what's the problem here? Why doesn't the whole equation explode in our faces?" Mr. Russo scanned the room, an inquiring look on his face. "Anybody? Don't all speak up at once!"

Jeffrey struggled to come up with the answer. Chemistry was hard enough as it was. Why did he have to have it last period, when his thoughts automatically started leaping forward to soccer practice? He could hardly pay attention.

The class laughed nervously as Mr. Russo arched his eyebrow. "Time's up," he said. "The key is the fact that the Avogadro number always remains constant."

Ava, Jeffrey began to write on his paper. Immediately he crossed it out and wrote *Avogo*, but that didn't look right either. His mind began to wander. He pictured Big Mesa's all-state left wing, Jack Everly, the one who had scored the winning goal against Sweet Valley last month. According to John Pfeifer, sports editor for *The Oracle*, Everly had twisted his knee two weeks ago and wouldn't be able to play in Saturday's game. If that was true, Sweet Valley would be a shoo-in.

Jeffrey's attention snapped back to the class. But by now the words coming out of Mr. Russo's mouth seemed to make no sense at all. *Terrific, Jeffrey*, he said to himself. *All you need now is to flunk chemistry.* A warning flashed through his head—one that had been issued to all soccer team members the week before. The administration had decided to monitor the grades of all varsity and junior varsity team members. Even one course grade below a C was enough to get a student suspended from a team.

Jeffrey gritted his teeth. If only they required a combined C average, he'd have no problem. He had mostly A's and B's in his other courses. But he was only hanging on by a thread in chemistry.

"Anyway," Mr. Russo was saying, "for those of you who are interested, I'll be staying late after school for any questions about Friday's exam."

The exam! Jeffrey had completely forgotten about it. *Perfect timing*, he thought. *The day before the biggest game of the year, and I'm going to be sweating it out over some hypothesis.*

At the sound of the bell, Jeffrey closed his notebook. Since it was only Monday, he would have plenty of time to prepare for the exam. He'd just have to try to catch up that night at home. Right now there was only one important thing, and that was soccer practice.

"And you guys on the soccer team," Mr. Russo called out over the commotion, "I know after school is tough for you this week, so if you want to see me during lunch, I can make arrangements."

"How about letting us take the test during lunch on Friday?" Tony Esteban asked. "We won't be able to concentrate last period!" A couple of other players called out in agreement.

Mr. Russo laughed. "Sorry, guys. I can't do that. Not that I don't think you're all honest . . ."

A groan went up from the players. "Come on, Mr. Russo, I guarantee we won't give away the questions," Tony said earnestly.

"Well, it's an unusual request, but I don't want to make things hard on you guys. I suppose if you all give me your word of honor . . ."

"All *right*!" Tony said. "Thanks, Mr. Russo. We really appreciate it."

At least Mr. Russo's a soccer fan, Jeffrey thought. *Maybe there's hope*. Wasting no time, he left the classroom and ran down the hall to his locker. He put everything except his chemistry books inside, then slammed it shut and turned toward the gym.

"He kicks . . . he scorrrrres!" came a voice from behind him. Jeffrey looked over his shoulder to see Ronnie approaching.

"Hey, Ronnie," Jeffrey said, backing down the hallway.

"You heading over to practice now?" Ronnie asked.

"Yeah." Jeffrey shrugged. "Otherwise, I'd stop and talk. See you later."

"I'll go with you!"

"Well, I'm kind of in a hurry." He quickened his step, but Ronnie trotted along beside him.

"You having some special prechampionship-game drills today?" Ronnie asked.

"Yeah," Jeffrey answered. "Coach Horner's going for broke. There'll be at least ten laps around the track for starters. Then some corner kick practice, dribbling around columns until we're dizzy, scrimmage, the works."

"You know, Jeff, you're a great team player. Did anyone ever tell you that?"

Jeffrey stopped in front of the gym door. "Yeah, thanks. Look, I'll talk to you later. Take it easy," he said, pushing the door open.

"You really were amazing in that game, you know."

"Thanks." *OK, enough already*, Jeffrey thought, walking into the gym.

"Wait!" Ronnie said. "Can I talk to you, Jeff, as a friend? It's really important."

Jeffrey looked up at the clock on the wall. "All right. But if I'm late for practice—"

"This'll only take a second," Ronnie promised. He led Jeffrey to a secluded spot near the bleachers and looked around nervously. Then he leaned closer and whispered, "I haven't told this to anyone yet, but I'm sort of in a little trouble."

"What is it, Ronnie? Are those jerks from the Dairi Burger bothering you again?"

"No, no, it's not that. It's . . . well, *financial* trouble. I was just wondering if you could lend me some money—"

"What?"

"Just until Saturday," Ronnie said quickly. "I swear it! All I need is, say, a hundred bucks."

Jeffrey looked at Ronnie as if he were crazy. "A hundred?"

"OK, fifty. It's just for a few days."

"What's going on, Ronnie? The other day you were throwing money around like crazy. And today you offer to loan Jessica a grand!"

"I know, I know," Ronnie said with a sigh. "I guess I just threw a little too much around. And by the time Jessica needs money, I'm sure I'll have it. It's just that I'm supposed to pay some business contacts in L.A. They usually don't collect until the end of the month, but one of them called me last night and said he wants the rest of his cash *tomorrow*, and there's no way I have the money."

"Hang on a second," Jeffrey said. "These business contacts of yours sound a little fishy to me."

Ronnie stared at the gym floor. "Well, you know, odds makers aren't exactly the world's most reasonable people."

"Odds makers? You mean bookies, don't you?"

"Well—yeah, if you want to put it that way."

"How much do they want from you, Ronnie? I can't believe they would be so desperate for fifty dollars. They can't wait till the weekend?" Jeffrey asked.

"Well," Ronnie said, "actually, it's more than just the fifty, but that's all I feel I can ask you for."

"How much do you really need, Ronnie?"

"Just, like, two grand or so," he mumbled.

Jeffrey's mouth dropped open in disbelief. "Two thousand?"

"It's not that bad, Jeff. I'm pretty sure I can hold him off with about five hundred. But don't worry, I have a few more friends I can count on. I'm going to borrow a little from each of them until the weekend. Then I'll be able to cash in my winnings and pay everybody back."

He smiled. "I just won't foot everyone's bill at the Dairi Burger this Saturday, that's all."

Jeffrey realized his teammates were probably on the field by now. He knew he should join them and say no to Ronnie, but he just couldn't send Ronnie away empty-handed, even if the money was for a bunch of crooks.

Jeffrey reached into his pocket. "Look, Ronnie, I don't have fifty, but I'll lend you what I do have, if you'll promise me something."

"Sure, sure. Whatever you want!"

Pulling out a couple of tens and a five, Jeffrey said, "After this weekend, think hard about giving up gambling. You know it's going to cause you nothing but trouble."

"I know. You're right," Ronnie said, taking the twenty-five dollars. "Thanks for the money, Jeff. You're a real buddy. I won't forget this."

"You'd better not!" Jeffrey said with a laugh. "That's supposed to last me through Saturday night!" With that, he darted into the locker room, hoping Coach Horner wouldn't be too angry.

After school that day, Jessica showed up early for her meeting at Treasure Island. She had raced home to redo her image for maximum effect. She had pulled back her hair, reapplied her makeup for a more sophisticated look that accentuated her cheekbones, and borrowed a sleek, pin-striped dress from her mother. She looked every bit the confident businesswoman; even Elizabeth had said so.

Now, as she smiled across the counter at the store manager, Jessica felt as if she could sell vacation land in Siberia if she wanted to. She put three small boxes on the jewelry counter and opened the first one. "*This* is the one I think will sell out first, Ms. Lussier. I've always had the best response with it."

She held the box up for the manager to see. Inside was the pair of earrings she had worn to the Dairi Burger the past Saturday.

Jessica watched the expression on Ms. Lussier's face. There wasn't a flicker of excitement in her eyes, nor a trace of a smile on her lips.

"They're—very heavy-looking," Ms. Lussier said slowly.

"I'm finding that heavy is *in* these days," Jessica replied, lifting the earrings out of the box.

Ms. Lussier just stared at her, obviously unconvinced. But Jessica wasn't bothered at all by the response. "Of course," she said, "it's really impossible to appreciate them when they're just sitting in the box like that."

With a big smile, Jessica put the earrings on. "There. What do you think?"

Ms. Lussier's eyebrows rose as she carefully

examined the earrings. *I've got her*, Jessica said to herself. *I knew this would do the trick.*

"Well," Ms. Lussier said, "I can see your point. They do look sort of interesting on you."

"Wow, look at those!" a voice rang out from behind Ms. Lussier. "I've never seen anything like them. I wonder if that's the last pair!"

Easy, Lila, Jessica thought. *Don't lay it on too thick.*

Lila and Amy walked over to Ms. Lussier, pretending not to know Jessica. "Excuse me. Do you have any more of those?" Amy asked.

"Well, uh, no, I don't," Ms. Lussier said.

Lila sighed with exasperation. "I *knew* it! Doesn't it figure? The nicest thing in here, and it's sold out!"

A smile crept across Ms. Lussier's face. "But we can order them for you."

Jessica beamed at her friends. She would be rich in no time!

The next day seemed to drag on forever for Ronnie. He couldn't wait to get to the Phi Epsilon meeting, where he'd finally be able to ask his friends to lend him some money. After all, Ronnie told himself, that was what being a fraternity brother was all about—helping out a friend in need.

While driving his car up to the Patman mansion after school, Ronnie was in a great mood. For the first time he didn't feel like an outsider puttering through Sweet Valley's exclusive hill section in an old Toyota. This time he was in Big Al's Mustang. At the head of the driveway, near the five-car garage, several cars were parked— mostly midsize, inexpensive sedans. All alone, to the right of the others, was Bruce's black Porsche. Grinning, Ronnie pulled up right behind it. *The quality cars have to stick together*, he thought.

When Ronnie stepped out of the car, he heard a loud rock beat coming from inside the enormous mansion. As he walked toward the front door, he looked around at the spacious grounds. No matter how many times Ronnie had been to the Patman mansion, no matter how many times he'd driven up that driveway and looked out over the spectacular view of Sweet Valley, he still couldn't help but be in awe. *This is how I want to live*, he said to himself. *No worries about money, the world at my feet.*

He remembered having the same excited feeling as he and his parents drove up to their split-level ranch when he was young. He shook his head as he thought about how things had changed. Now that he and his father were fighting all the time, the place seemed way too small. Mr. Edwards knew all about Big Al, and he was furious with

Ronnie for getting involved with a bookie. Ronnie couldn't make him understand that Big Al was going to be their ticket to a better life.

Ronnie knocked on the front door, and the Patmans' maid answered. She led him to a basement room.

"Hey, Ronnie, where have you been?" Winston Egbert called out as Ronnie entered. Winston was sitting near the door, and as far as Ronnie could tell, no one else had seen or heard him come in.

"Hi, Winston. Can I talk to you a second before the meeting starts?" Ronnie asked him.

"Sure," Winston answered. "What's up?"

Ronnie was glad that he had seen Winston first. Of all the Phi Epsilon brothers, Winston was probably the friendliest and most understanding. If any of them could be counted on, it was him. "Well, I was wondering if you could front me a few bucks until Saturday. I'm sort of stuck."

Winston gave him a baffled look. "Hey, what is this? Last Saturday I overheard you telling a girl you'd buy her the Beverly Hills Hotel for her birthday!"

Ronnie smiled self-consciously at Winston's joke. "I guess I overdid it a little. Hey, it's not like I'm broke or anything. I'm just having a few cash-flow problems."

Suddenly Ronnie became aware of Bruce Patman standing right behind him. " 'Cash-flow problems'?" Bruce said in a sneering tone. "Don't tell me you blew your entire fortune at the Dairi Burger!"

"No, I didn't *blow* it," Ronnie insisted. He hoped Bruce wouldn't make a big deal about the whole thing in front of everybody.

"I just need to raise a few hundred bucks— temporarily," Ronnie continued. Now Tom McKay, Michael Harris, and Bill Chase were all looking at him and grinning. *This is incredible*, he thought. *They don't believe me!* "Look, it's for a good reason, and I guarantee I'll pay every-body back on Saturday. Now, I need about four hundred seventy-five, so if everybody could give me a few bucks . . ."

"Right, Ronnie," Bruce said with a smirk. "But first I'll have to consult my financial ad-viser. I'll get back to you next week. Maybe we can do lunch."

Tom McKay just rolled his eyes and walked over to the stereo, followed by Michael Harris.

"Sorry, Ronnie," Winston said. "I just took a weekend job, and it doesn't really pay much."

Bill Chase shrugged halfheartedly. "I'm broke, too."

A wave of panic shot through Ronnie. "Come on," he pleaded. "How about just twenty or twenty-five bucks?"

No one answered him.

Some fraternity, he thought. *I get more "brother-hood" from people I barely know.* He reached into his pocket and fingered the twenty-five dollars Jeffrey had given him. It didn't look like he was going to get much more than that.

He checked his watch. It was already 5:00, the time he had arranged to call Big Al. After making an excuse about having to get something out of his car, he trudged back upstairs to the front hallway, then went over to the phone near the stairs and quickly dialed the number.

"Yeah?" A voice on the other end barked.

"This is Smallfry, calling Big Al," Ronnie said softly, using the code name he and Big Al had agreed on.

"You got the money, kid?" the voice demanded.

Ronnie tried to sound cheerful. "Big Al? Hey, I didn't recognize your voice at first. Since when are you picking up your own phone?"

"Cut the small talk. I asked you a question."

"Well, uh, unfortunately, I had an unforeseen dilemma in the collection process—"

"Look, I ain't impressed by the five-dollar words. I want it straight. Are you telling me you don't got it?"

"As a matter of fact—"

"Yes or no, kid. It's a simple question."

Ronnie gulped. He was happy about only

one thing: that he wasn't talking to Big Al face-to-face. "I have some of it," he said weakly.

"*'Some'*? How much is 'some'?"

"Um, twenty-five dollars?"

"Twenty-five!" Big Al's voice was so loud that Ronnie was afraid the Patmans' maid would hear it. "I'm a patient man, Smallfry," he said, his voice seething with rage. "It takes a lot to get me rattled. But you know what? You ought to be kissing the ground, kid. 'Cause if I were right there this minute, you would be wallpaper. Understood?"

"Understood!" Ronnie blurted. "Listen, Big Al, this was just a fluke! I'm good for the money. I'll pay you after the weekend, I promise. If there's any other way I can make this up to you, just tell me!"

There was a chilling silence at the other end. When Big Al finally spoke, his voice was soft and composed. "You're in luck, Smallfry. In fact, right now you are the luckiest twerp in California."

"Wh-what do you mean?" Ronnie asked.

Big Al chuckled. "I just thought of a way for you to make this up to me, kid. But I don't think you're going to like it."

"Like it?" he said. "Don't worry about that, Big Al. Just tell me, I'll do anything!" Ronnie felt as if a light had opened up at the end of a long, dark tunnel.

He leaned against the wall and listened quietly as Big Al laid out his plan. Slowly he felt his face turning pale. It was impossible . . . insane!

But from the tone of Big Al's voice, Ronnie knew he didn't have a choice. He had to do it, no matter what.

Five

Jessica actually felt a little nervous as she walked through the mall toward Treasure Island on Wednesday. It was only two days after she had dropped off her samples, and already Ms. Lussier had left a message at the Wakefields' saying that she wanted to meet with Jessica.

She paused in front of the store, discreetly examining her reflection in the glass window. The display had been changed slightly since Monday, and there was a small Position Available sign posted at eye level. *To help with the increased demand for the Wakefield line*, she added silently.

Smiling, Jessica breezed into the store and walked up to the salesgirl at the counter. "I'd like to see Ms. Lussier, please," she said, trying to sound businesslike.

"Is that Jessica Wakefield?" Ms. Lussier's voice called out from the back of the shop.

"Yes," Jessica answered.

"Well, hello! If it isn't my budding designer," Ms. Lussier said, emerging from behind a set of display shelves. She gave Jessica a wide, friendly smile. "You look wonderful, as always!"

"Hello, Ms. Lussier. It's nice to see you." Jessica was taken aback for a moment. This was a far cry from the cool reception she had received on Monday.

"I have good news for you. Look." Ms. Lussier gestured toward a black felt pad inside a glass case where two sets of Jessica's earrings and one of her necklaces were displayed. "I have to admit," she said, "I wasn't so sure these would sell. But now I'm sorry you only gave me eight pieces. We had a flurry of purchases, both yesterday and today. The girls seem to go wild over them."

"I'm so happy to hear that," Jessica said. "But I'm not too surprised. I've had great compliments on those pieces whenever I've worn them."

"Well, it just goes to show," Ms. Lussier replied. "You never can predict what teenagers are going to like. Anyway, why don't you come on back to my office? We have a lot to talk about."

As Ms. Lussier led the way, Jessica surveyed the store. *What I'll need is a nice little display section of my own*, she thought, eyeing a collection of designer jewelry near the front of the store. *Maybe I'll have someone design a Wakefield logo to put above it.*

"Have a seat," Ms. Lussier said when they stepped inside her office. She sat down behind a small mahogany desk that was covered with papers. "Now, from everything I've seen about you, I can tell you're serious about your business."

"Very serious," Jessica said, sitting forward with just the right combination of eagerness and confidence. "I've been working on my designs and marketing strategies in my spare time and I'm convinced there's a niche for my creations." *Not bad*, she said to herself, pleased to have remembered the sales pitch she had practiced.

"Well, you may be right. But, of course, you realize it takes years to establish a reputation, and maybe one in a thousand really makes it big."

Jessica nodded. "Well, all the successful people have to start somewhere, don't they?"

"Exactly. And I'd like to give you the opportunity to find out if you're one of them." Ms. Lussier smiled. "Treasure Island would love to be known as the store that gave a hot young designer her start. Will you take an order for more jewelry?"

Hot young designer. The words made Jessica ngle with excitement. "I'd love to, Ms. Lussier. low many items would you like?"

"Well . . ." Ms. Lussier leaned back and rossed one leg over the other. "How many do ou have? I might just take them all."

Jessica was stunned by Ms. Lussier's offer. *tay cool,* she said to herself. *Don't let on that you on't have anything stocked up. That would be in-redibly unprofessional.* "Um, well, I'll have to heck my reserves," she hedged.

"Fine. Don't be afraid to bring everything. 'll display what I can and store the rest. Also, I'd like to get these from you as soon as ossible. Once something catches on, it's good o be well stocked so that you don't sell out. f we sell as much as I expect we will, I'll lace periodic orders with you. What do you hink, Jessica? Are those terms satisfactory?"

"Yes, thank you. It sounds great!" Jessica ried not to sound overwhelmed.

Ms. Lussier stood up and extended her and. "It's a deal, young lady. I hope for oth of our sakes that the line is a smashing uccess."

"Me, too," Jessica said, rising from her seat nd shaking Ms. Lussier's hand. "I'll be in touch vith you soon."

Jessica tried to look calm and composed as

she walked out the door, but she was so excited
she could hardly feel the ground beneath her
feet.

"You mean he actually threatened you over
the phone?" Jeffrey asked, leaning against his
locker after soccer practice that day.

"It was like something out of a bad movie,"
Ronnie answered. "Just thinking about it kept
me up all last night."

"I don't blame you." Jeffrey opened his locker
and took out his varsity jacket. "If you ask me,
the guy sounds like a lot of hot air. I mean, it's
already Wednesday. I'm sure he can afford to
hold off until the weekend for his money. I
can't mean that much to him."

"You don't know these guys, Jeff. They're
ruthless. There's no way I could stall him."

"So what's he going to do? Gun you down
on the school steps?" Jeffrey joked. "Be serious."

"Actually, he did say there was a way to call
off all my debts," Ronnie said.

"Of course there is. What did he say?"

"Well . . . that's what I wanted to talk to you
about."

Jeffrey shook his head. "Sorry, Ronnie. I gave
you all I could—"

"No, no! It has nothing to do with money.
You'd just have to do me one really small favor."

"What kind of a favor?" Jeffrey asked, starting to get suspicious.

"Can we talk about it on the way home?"

"Well, no. I'm supposed to meet Elizabeth here. We're going to leave together," Jeffrey told him.

Ronnie looked around. "Can we talk over there, then?" he said, pointing to a dark corner at the end of the hall.

"Sure," Jeffrey said with a shrug. By now he knew that when Ronnie wanted something, he wouldn't take no for an answer.

Jeffrey took his backpack out of his locker, closed it, then walked with Ronnie to the corner. After looking both ways, Ronnie took a deep breath. "OK, I'll get right to the point. You guys are a big favorite to win the game on Saturday. There's no question in my mind that you guys will—you're great! Now, obviously, in terms of betting, the big money would be on the underdog winning. But that's not the only kind of bet that can pay off." Ronnie paused for a minute.

Jeffrey's eyes widened in disbelief. "I don't believe what you're saying. Are you asking me to throw the game?"

"Throw the game? No, Jeff, of course not! I was just trying to say that a lot of money could be made by betting on the *point* spread. In other words, not will Sweet Valley win, but by how much—"

"I understand point spread," Jeffrey snapped.

"OK. So what I'm saying is, all I need to do is guarantee that the Gladiators will win by two points. I don't know if you realize it, but you guys became *four*-point favorites when Jack Everly was injured. After all, he's the Bulldogs' top scorer. But if I can place a few big bets and guarantee they'll be winning ones, I'll have it made. My contract will be paid back, and you can be sure there'll be something in it for you. All you have to do is win! By two points," Ronnie added, reminding Jeffrey of his request.

A horrible feeling welled up inside Jeffrey. He stared at Ronnie as his mind searched for the words to express his shock. "In other words, you want me to sabotage my team."

Ronnie shook his head vigorously. "No, I wouldn't dream of asking you to do that! In fact, if the game really *is* close, you may not have to do a thing! All I'm asking is that you *lay back* a little, maybe play just a fraction less hard than usual—but only if necessary! I mean, what's the difference between a two-point win and a slaughter? Either way you've got the championship!" he said frantically.

"Nothing doing," Jeffrey said flatly. He walked away from Ronnie, disgusted by the whole situation.

Suddenly he felt Ronnie's hand clutching his arm. "Jeff, please. Promise me you'll at least think about it!"

Jeffrey yanked his arm away. He felt every muscle in his body stiffen with tension. "Look, if you want to do something illegal, it's your business. But if you think you're going to drag me into it, you've got the wrong guy. And if I even see you near any of my teammates—"

"But I'm not asking you to do anything illegal," Ronnie protested, interrupting him.

"No kidding," Jeffrey shot back. "It's only *dishonest*, right? You want me to betray my team. Sorry, Ronnie, that's just not the way I do things. Besides, if you're so concerned about raising money, why don't you sell your car?"

Ronnie lowered his eyes. "It's not mine," he admitted softly. "Big Al has several, cars and he lent one to me. The way things are going, I don't know why he hasn't taken it back."

"Well, I'm sorry to hear that, Ronnie," Jeffrey said. He slung his backpack over his shoulder. "I guess you'll have to work that out with him. Look, I'll see you later."

"You can't do this to me!" Ronnie said, practically shouting. His face was white with fear. "You're my only chance," he pleaded.

"You know what your only chance to get out of this is, Ronnie? Your only chance is to kiss this Al creep goodbye. As long as you're tied to him, you're going to be in trouble."

"You're right," Ronnie said. "That's exactly what I plan to do after this weekend. I know I'm in too deep, and I've had enough." He looked up with tear-filled eyes. "But you have to understand, right now I need help."

Jeffrey was still outraged, but Ronnie's pathetic look had softened him slightly. "Look," he said calmly, "all I can suggest is to give the guy what you can now and work the rest out after the weekend. Find another way to pay him back. I'm sure there must be something you could do."

Ronnie shook his head listlessly. In a soft, almost inaudible voice, he said, "You don't understand. If I can't guarantee this, I may not *make* it to the weekend."

Elizabeth quickly slipped out the door of the *Oracle* office. The staff meeting had run longer than expected, and she had told Jeffrey she would meet him at his locker ten minutes ago.

As she turned the corner and walked down the hall toward his locker, she saw that he wasn't there. She sighed with disappointment. *Maybe he got bored and left*, she thought.

Just then she heard muffled voices from around the corner at the end of the hallway.

"You mean he really means it?"

Elizabeth's mood brightened at the sound of Jeffrey's voice, and she quickened her pace.

"Yes. I know it's hard to believe, but these guys really take this stuff seriously. It's their life!"

Elizabeth stopped walking. The second voice belonged to Ronnie Edwards.

"Look," Ronnie continued, "don't say no yet. Just think about it. It's not that bad a thing to do. Besides, you promised you'd never tell anyone, right? So no one besides us will ever know!"

What is he talking about? Elizabeth wondered. Whatever it was, she didn't like the sound of it.

She hurried around the corner, hoping to stop whatever strange plot Ronnie was trying to involve Jeffrey in. Jeffrey's back was turned to her, and he was speaking to Ronnie in an exasperated voice.

"Look, all I can tell you is I'll think about it. But I can't promise you anything. It's—"

"Oh, *hi*, Elizabeth!" Ronnie called out in a loud voice, obviously trying to cut off Jeffrey before he revealed anything important.

Jeffrey spun around, and his face broke into a grin. "Hey, Liz!" Turning back to Ronnie, he said, "Take it easy. I'll talk to you tomorrow."

"You guys need a ride home?" Ronnie asked. "My car's parked out back."

"No, thanks. I have my car, too," Elizabeth said. "Besides, I haven't been to my locker yet."

"OK, see you." As Ronnie walked away from Elizabeth and Jeffrey, toward the back exit of the school, he called over his shoulder, "Maybe I'll give you a call tonight, Jeff?"

"All right." Jeffrey fell silent as he and Elizabeth walked through the lobby.

"What was that all about?" Elizabeth asked.

"What was what all about?"

"I couldn't help overhearing you guys when I was walking down the hallway. What does Ronnie want you to think about?"

Jeffrey frowned and kept looking straight ahead. "Oh, nothing important."

"OK," she said, trying not to sound hurt. Elizabeth didn't know why Jeffrey was acting so secretive if it was nothing. She had a feeling that he and Ronnie were trying to keep something from her for some reason.

After a brief stop at her locker, Elizabeth and Jeffrey walked out to the parking lot and climbed into the red Fiat convertible that the twins shared. As Elizabeth started the car, Jeffrey stared silently ahead, apparently deep in thought.

Over the car radio an announcer's voice crackled: "Looking ahead to Saturday, we may see a cooling trend, with possible showers in the early afternoon. . . ."

Elizabeth winced. "Uh-oh. That's too bad."

"What is?" Jeffrey said.

"The weather. Didn't you hear that, Jeffrey? It might rain for the big game."

"Sorry." Jeffrey shrugged. "I wasn't listening."

Elizabeth was about to back out of her parking space, but instead she kept the gear shift in park and turned to Jeffrey. "What's wrong? I *know* something's on your mind. Can't you talk to me about it?"

"It's nothing, Liz. Really," he insisted.

Elizabeth rolled her eyes. "You're being silly, Jeffrey. Something Ronnie said upset you, didn't it?"

"No—it's not that."

"Then what is it?"

"I told you, it's nothing." Jeffrey stretched his legs out and shifted in his seat. "I guess I'm just extra keyed up this week. I mean, with the game coming up, and this chemistry exam . . . I have no idea what Mr. Russo's talking about half the time! And if I flunk out, they're not going to let me play soccer next season."

Elizabeth leaned over and kissed Jeffrey on the cheek. "Don't worry, you're going to do fine. I'll drive you right home, and you can study all night."

"That's another thing," Jeffrey said with a sigh. "Ronnie's going to call tonight, probably right when I'm studying."

"Well, you don't have to worry about that," Elizabeth said. "You don't have to talk to him for long if you don't want to. Just tell him you're busy studying."

"Well, he *is* a friend . . ."

"If he's a friend, Jeffrey, he'll understand that you're busy. *I'm* not going to bother you this week, am I? I know you've got too much on your mind."

Jeffrey laughed. "Yeah, but how would you feel if you called and I said I couldn't talk to you?"

"I'd feel terrible, but I'd understand. Besides, we're talking about *Ronnie*," Elizabeth pointed out, raising her voice. "You barely know him. How can he expect you to drop everything for him?"

"OK, OK, I won't talk to him!" Jeffrey said, holding up his hands in defeat. "I don't know why you're so hung up about Ronnie, Liz."

"I'm not 'hung up,' " Elizabeth said, feeling exasperated. "But to tell you the truth, it seems strange that he's hanging around you all the time. You guys don't have that much in common, and *you* have a lot of other things to do—not to mention other friends to hang out with. You know, Jeffrey, there is such a thing as spreading yourself too thin."

"I told you I'm not going to talk to him!"

Jeffrey snapped, sitting back in his seat. "And it's really stupid for us to let Ronnie cause a fight between us. Let's get going. I want to at least *look* at my chem notebook before dinner."

Without a word, Elizabeth backed out of the space. As she maneuvered out of the lot toward the street, she struggled to fight back tears.

Jeffrey's right, it is stupid to let Ronnie come between us, Elizabeth thought. *But if he really believes that, then why is he letting it happen?*

Six

"It's only Thursday, guys," Coach Horner said, pacing back and forth in the locker room. "You guys are acting like the season is already over. You think the championship trophy is in the bag, just because Jack Everly is injured!" He scanned the faces of the Sweet Valley High team, letting his words sink in. "Well, judging from the way you played today, I don't think you're going to have anything to add to your trophy shelves!"

Jeffrey was sitting next to Aaron on a wooden bench, pretending to pay attention to Coach Horner's speech. But in reality, other images were flashing through his mind: the hurt look on Elizabeth's face, the panic in Ronnie's voice . . .

Despite his promise to Elizabeth, Jeffrey had taken Ronnie's call the night before. Now the conversation was haunting him. The whole time

Ronnie had been practically hysterical. He said he'd just talked to Big Al, who had threatened him again—something about getting one of his men after him. Jeffrey had tried to calm him down, but Ronnie had only gotten more and more frantic by the end of the conversation when Jeffrey had told him he couldn't help him out. The rest of the evening Jeffrey had hardly been able to concentrate on chemistry.

What is it about this guy? Jeffrey asked himself. *It's not as if he's my best friend or anything! Besides, he got himself into this.* The suggestion to lay back during the championship game was ridiculous, out of the question. His whole life Jeffrey had been brought up to believe that honesty and hard work were the only ways to get ahead. When he was a kid, just starting to play sports, his father had told him, "Honor your family, honor your friends, and honor your teammates." At the time Jeffrey had thought it was kind of corny. But he had lived by it his whole life, and he wasn't about to stop. He couldn't conceive of doing something as immoral as fixing a game.

Then why was he still thinking about it?

"I want you guys to fight for this championship as if your lives depended on it," Coach Horner continued. "Push everything else to the back of your mind and tell yourself this is the most important game you've ever played."

Any other time Jeffrey would have felt his

blood start to pound with excitement. But that day Coach Horner's words sounded hollow and distant. Jeffrey realized he'd *always* played as if his life depended on it, always put everything else aside for soccer.

And what good had it done him? A classmate of his, someone who was really counting on him, was in deep trouble. What if Big Al's threats *were* serious? What if Ronnie was seriously hurt, just because the Sweet Valley Gladiators won by three points instead of two?

And that was only part of the problem. Not only might he be putting Ronnie in jeopardy, but now Elizabeth was angry at him. Jeffrey's whole "code of honor" was backfiring. How could he honor Ronnie's wish to keep his plan a secret without being dishonest to Elizabeth? And how could he be loyal to his teammates in the game on Saturday without being being disloyal to Ronnie? Jeffrey was so confused he wanted to scream.

When Coach Horner finished talking, Jeffrey ran out onto the field with the other players, anxious to get some of his anger out through exercise. A soccer ball headed his way from the foot of Brad Tomasi. Jeffrey trapped it skillfully and sent it flying just wide of the goal.

"All right!" Coach Horner's voice boomed through a bullhorn. "Let's have the junior varsity against the varsity. Line up!"

Jeffrey took his position on the center line. At the sound of the coach's whistle, Chris Wells, a junior varsity forward, took control of the ball.

Jeffrey didn't know Chris very well, but he could tell he was going to be a good varsity player someday. He had sharp reflexes, and there was a look of fierce determination in his eyes. When he glanced at Jeffrey momentarily, the defiant look on his face relayed the message: *Don't even try to take this ball away from me.*

There was something about that attitude that struck Jeffrey as excessive. *Is that what I look like when I play?* Jeffrey wondered. In that split second he felt himself slow down and lose a step on Chris.

Chris's eyes flickered brightly as he saw a sudden opportunity. With a lightning-quick move, he dribbled right past Jeffrey and took a shot on goal.

"Score!" Coach Horner yelled through his bullhorn.

Jeffrey turned around just in time to see Chris raise his arms in victory. The goalie was standing with his hands on his hips, staring in Jeffrey's direction with an aggravated look on his face.

"Not bad, Wells!" Michael Schmidt called out. "You really faked him out!"

Walking around briskly in a circle, Chris flashed a brief, triumphant smile at Jeffrey.

OK, that did it, Jeffrey said to himself, feeling his temples pounding from the humiliation. *Forget about Ronnie Edwards and his problems. I have to play my best. I don't know any other way.*

"No, Mom, this isn't going to be like Tofu-Glo, I just know it!"

Am I ever going to live that down? Jessica said to herself. One of her previous business experiments, selling soybean–based cosmetics, had resulted in a garage full of rotting makeup and shampoo that no one had wanted to buy.

Mrs. Wakefield gave her daughter a wry smile. "How many times have I heard *those* words before?" She dropped her leather bag onto a kitchen chair and adjusted the shoulder pads of her cream-colored silk blouse. With her blond pageboy haircut and slim waistline, Alice Wakefield could have passed for Jessica's older sister.

"But you yourself said we all have to learn from our mistakes," Jessica reasoned. "Just because I screwed up once doesn't mean I should stop trying. Didn't you ever do some silly things when you were getting started in business?"

Mrs. Wakefield laughed. "Why did I *know* you were going to turn the tables on me like that?" she said. "I guess I did have my share—like the time I designed the living room of one of your dad's old law partners and gave the wallpaper measurements to the factory in square feet instead of square yards." She grinned. "They ended up using it to paper the bathroom."

"Really?" Jessica said, giggling. Inside, she was thinking, *Good, I knew that would work.*

"Yes, really," Mrs. Wakefield said with a sigh. "But that's not the point, Jess. I'm just not sure you realize what you're up against. The jewelry market is tough. Fads come and go, and there are so many designers out there competing for attention."

"I know, Mom, but I'm not trying to become world-famous or anything. I just think the time is right for these designs. The girls in school love them." She looked her mother squarely in the eye. "All I want is to see if I can do it, Mom. I know it may not work, but whether or not it does, I'll still have a valuable experience."

Mrs. Wakefield seemed to be considering Jessica's argument. For a moment or two she didn't say a word. Then she raised one eyebrow and looked at her daughter warily. "OK, how much is all this going to cost?"

Bubbling with excitement, Jessica reached into her bag and took out a sheet of paper she had been scribbling on. "It all depends on how many I make. I figure I should give Ms. Lussier—she's the manager of Treasure Island—about ten more pieces."

"Ten? Does she want that many?"

"She said she'd take as many as I could give her."

"Wow!" Mrs. Wakefield said. "That's great."

"I called a wholesaler today. The only problem is, the prices are high if you only order a few things—compared to if you order in bulk, I mean. And even though most of the pieces will be costume jewelry, I figured I'd like to go upscale with a few others—like put in some semi-precious stones, maybe do some gold-plated settings. Anyway, the stones really drive the price up, so I'm sort of figuring on an average of twenty or twenty-five dollars per piece."

Jessica waited for her mother to react. Mrs. Wakefield nodded slowly. "So you're talking about a lot of money, aren't you?"

"Yes, I guess so. But I could easily sell everything at a fifty percent markup, which means—"

"You'd have to sell about seven out of the ten to break even," Mrs. Wakefield said.

"Well, that's if I only make ten pieces. The wholesale prices really drop if I order more," Jessica argued.

Mrs. Wakefield shook her head. "No, you don't want to get in over your head, Jess. Start with the ten pieces." She smiled. "I'll help you get started with a two-hundred-dollar loan—"

Before she could finish, Jessica threw her arms around her. "Thanks, Mom! You are the absolute *best*—"

66

"Whoa! Hold on, there!" Mrs. Wakefield interrupted. "Don't forget, this is a *loan*. I'm expecting that money back when you start selling your jewelry."

"Of course!" Jessica was practically jumping with excitement. "Mom, I'll never forget this. When I'm rich and famous, I'll buy you a dream office that you can design however you want."

"OK, it's a deal." Smiling, Mrs. Wakefield put an arm around Jessica's shoulder. "But first, how about helping me design some salad for dinner?"

"Sure." Jessica quickly consulted her watch. "Just let me call to order some supplies before the warehouse closes. It's almost six o'clock."

Jessica ran upstairs to her bedroom, closed the door behind her, and flicked on the light switch. Then she flopped down onto a pile of clothes on her bed and reached under a throw pillow for the phone. Leaning over, she pulled the dog-eared Sweet Valley phone book out from under her bed.

She quickly leafed through it, then suddenly stopped. *I have to sell seven items to break even*, she thought. That seemed like a lot, especially if she would have to pay her mother back with the profits. She sat up and grabbed a jewelry catalog that was lying on her night table, then fished out a pen and a calculator from her bag. She began figuring out her profit. She sat back and looked at the figure. Not bad, but not fantastic, either.

Ms. Lussier's words came back to her: "How many do you have? I might just take them all." Remembering some of the figures she had been quoted over the phone by the wholesaler, Jessica calculated what would happen if she doubled her order.

Her eyes widened when she realized that her profits would shoot up dramatically if she sold them all. And if she tripled or quadrupled the order! . . . She might be able to swing it if the wholesaler would accept monthly payments. That way she could pay them *after* she started making money.

Her fingers flew over the buttons of the calculator. Jessica began to smile. She imagined flying first-class to the Caribbean for spring break, with a new designer bathing suit for each day of the week, on a plane full of gorgeous guys vying for her attention. Her new life was about to begin!

Jessica pored through the directory for the phone number of Classic Land Imports, the supplier she would be ordering from.

She quickly dialed, crossing the fingers of her other hand for good luck.

"Classic Land, Stuart speaking," a voice answered.

"Oh, hi, Stuart!" Jessica said cheerfully. "I've

spoken to you before. My name is Jessica Wakefield."

"Right!" Stuart said. "You're the girl who wanted the feathers and the stones. I remember. Are you ready to place an order?"

"Uh, yes," Jessica answered, looking at her list of materials. "I'd like three boxes of white beads, three boxes of black . . ."

"Three *faux* pearls, three *faux* onyx," he repeated her order back to her. "And?"

"Also, I'll take thirty-five of your size three rhinestones."

"Mmm. That's an odd lot. It means splitting up a carton. You're better off price-wise if you order fifty."

"All right, make it fifty. And four small Ceylon sapphires—"

"We just got in a beautiful shipment of lighter blue ones," he interrupted. "They're a little more expensive, but the profit margin is much greater, and the price goes down in lots of six." Stuart paused. "I hope you don't mind my suggestions, Jessica."

"No, no. They're really good ideas!" she told him.

It took Jessica about fifteen minutes to order the rest of her materials. It was a much larger order than she had expected to make, but the prices were simply too good to resist. She was going to make a fortune, anyway, so what did it matter?

Finally Jessica sighed and said, "OK, I think that'll keep me busy for a while. I just hope I can sell everything."

"Well, the materials are the highest quality," Stuart assured her. "It's only a matter of the design."

"Only!" Jessica laughed. "Actually, I'm pretty sure I've got some good ideas. Now, how much will this order cost, Stuart?" She doodled on her notepad and braced herself for the figure.

"Just a second." Jessica could hear the faint clacking and whirr of an adding machine in the background. "All right, with sales tax, it comes to nine hundred eight dollars and ten cents."

Jessica suppressed a small gasp. Suddenly her mother's loan didn't even seem like much of a down payment. For a moment she thought of canceling the whole thing.

But a little voice inside of her kept telling her to go for it. After all, big success only came from taking big risks. Besides, if the line sold well, paying back that $200 would be no problem.

"Do you accept monthly payments?" Jessica asked.

"Well," Stuart said, sounding reluctant, "we prefer cash in full, but we'll take a major credit card."

"Oh," Jessica replied. That was something

she didn't have—yet. But maybe she could charm Stuart into letting her have the supplies some other way.

Then Jessica remembered something: Ronnie Edwards had offered to lend her some money. He had even mentioned the figure—"a grand or so," he had said.

He also said the offer would be there when I needed it, Jessica thought. *And that's now!*

"Still there, Jessica? What'll it be?" Stuart prompted. "Cash or charge?"

Jessica took a deep breath. "Cash," she told him.

"OK. Everything you ordered is in stock, so you can come by anytime. We'll close tomorrow at six as usual."

"Great! I'll see you tomorrow!" Jessica said. "Cash in hand!"

Seven

"You're cutting it close, aren't you?" Mr. Edwards said to Ronnie, looking up from the kitchen table on Friday morning.

"Yeah, Dad. I couldn't sleep last night," Ronnie replied as he stood in the kitchen doorway. He knew he looked awful. His hair was all bunched up on one side, and his face had a thin red crease on it, from sleeping on a wrinkle in his pillow.

Mr. Edwards looked at Ronnie with serious, penetrating eyes. "You didn't have insomnia until you got mixed up with that Remsen character, you know. I think you should—"

"Bye, Dad. I really have to go," Ronnie interrupted. He stumbled out of the room, tucking in his shirt as he went.

On the one hand, Ronnie was relieved it was Friday. If he had insomnia again tomorrow or the next day, at least he could sleep late. On the other hand, he dreaded the fact that it was one day closer to Saturday. Every time he thought about the soccer game, a chill ran down his spine. Who knew if Jeffrey was going to listen to him? And even if he did, how could Ronnie expect Jeffrey to control the scoring all by himself, especially now with rumors that Jack Everly, the Big Mesa star, was going to play after all.

I probably should have talked to Aaron Dallas or Mike Schmidt, too, Ronnie said to himself.

Hopping into the Mustang, he turned on the radio full blast, backed out of the driveway, and then took off down the street. He had already gotten into trouble twice that week for being late to homeroom, and he had no intention of making it three times.

Behind him he heard the screeching of tires. He looked into his mirror and saw a silver Lincoln Continental approaching at top speed.

He slowed down. *Just what I need*, he thought. *An unmarked police car.*

As he turned onto the road to Sweet Valley High, the car kept following him, but there was no siren, no voice over a bullhorn telling him to pull over, nothing to indicate that it was the police.

Ronnie made sure to signal as he switched from the left to the right lane. The Continental pulled into the right lane behind him, cutting off another car. The driver honked to indicate his displeasure.

What's going on here? Ronnie asked himself. He felt beads of sweat forming on his brow. When Sweet Valley High came into view on the right, he pulled into a parking space along the curb and turned off the engine. He watched as the Continental drove past him and stopped in front of the school.

Come on, Ronnie, don't be so paranoid. It's probably just somebody's parents in a hurry to get to work.

The driver's door of the Continental swung open, and a big, black-haired man with sunglasses and a suede jacket stepped out. Ronnie froze as the man started walking toward him.

This wasn't anyone's father. Ronnie took a deep breath, trying to calm himself. There was something in the man's smile that was very phony—and menacing.

Ronnie switched his ignition back on so that he would be ready to take off if necessary. Suddenly the man started running toward him, his expression fierce.

Ronnie yanked the steering wheel to the left. His tires squealed as he made a U-turn and sped away.

Ronnie's face blanched when he looked in his

mirror. The Continental had made a U-turn, too, and was catching up to him, fast.

Just ahead, Ronnie spotted an entrance ramp to the freeway. He angled onto the ramp without even touching his brakes. He barreled onto the freeway, his speedometer registering fifty . . . fifty-five . . . sixty . . .

As he came over the top of a hill, Ronnie saw the gray-blue ocean stretched out right in front of him. His stomach clenched with fear. A sign on his right said, End of Freeway/All Lanes Exit to Beach Road.

Of course, I should have gone east! Ronnie scolded himself. Now he had nowhere to go, and the Continental was practically behind him.

Ronnie raced down the freeway exit ramp and right into a traffic jam. Horns blared as the light at the end of the ramp turned yellow.

There was no way Ronnie could make the light. He pulled the car onto the grassy shoulder. His only hope was to get out and run to the beach. He threw open his door and stepped out.

But the stranger was right behind him. Before Ronnie could run, the man reached out, grabbing Ronnie's arm in a viselike grip, then jerked him backward.

"Not so fast," the gravelly voice threatened.

Ronnie spun around. The driver of the Continental was staring at him impassively through his dark sunglasses. He pushed Ronnie across the street toward the beach.

"Wh-who are you?" Ronnie asked. "What are you doing with me?" He looked at the other cars anxiously, hoping someone would notice that he was being dragged against his will.

"Just act natural, pretend that nothing's wrong," the man said as they walked along the beach. "I wouldn't suggest trying to call for help. It could be dangerous to your health."

The boardwalk cast an ominous shadow overhead as the man pushed Ronnie toward a dark, deserted spot underneath it.

"Y-you work for B-Big Al, right?" Ronnie stammered, stumbling on the sand. "Look, I told Big Al I was going to make good on my promise! You just have to give me till Satur—*oof!*"

Ronnie doubled over as the man gave him a swift punch in the abdomen and then hurled him against one of the wooden pillars.

"Please," Ronnie begged through gritted teeth. "Don't hurt me!"

He stared up into the man's granitelike face. In a deep, ominous voice that sent a chill through Ronnie, the man replied, "This is just a *friendly* message from your Uncle Al, kid. Let's just call it a sample of what will happen if you don't make good!"

* * *

On Fridays the Sweet Valley High cafeteria was always a lot noisier than usual, with high-pitched preweekend excitement. Jeffrey was taking his chemistry test, so Elizabeth was having lunch with Enid and Olivia Davidson, the arts editor for *The Oracle*. They had gotten to the cafeteria late, and the only three seats together were at the end of a long table where Jessica was sitting with her friends. Elizabeth hoped she wouldn't have to listen to another discussion of Jessica's earrings. But it was hopeless. That was *all* Jessica could talk about.

"I hate to say this," Enid whispered to Elizabeth with a sly look, "but those earrings look ridiculous."

Elizabeth tried to suppress a giggle. Amy, Cara, and Lila were all wearing Jessica-designed earrings. "Come on, Enid. They're just trying to support Jessica," Olivia said sympathetically.

"Must be tough. I'm sure it's hard enough just supporting those earrings," Enid commented.

"Stop it!" Elizabeth said with a smile, stirring her yogurt with a spoon. Looking at Jessica's enthusiastic expression, her twin found it hard not to admire her. When she wanted something, Jessica went after it. And who knew? Maybe this time—just *maybe*—a business scheme of her sister's might work!

". . . then I figure maybe about ten of the *faux* pearl necklaces, just to appeal to the more conservative types," Jessica was saying. "That rounds out the collection!"

"I don't know, Jessica," Lila said. "Do you really think they're going to take *that* many?"

Jessica rolled her eyes. "Well, I don't have to give Ms. Lussier all of them right away. First I'll just give her a few, let my reputation build. But at least I'll have the material handy when I want to make more." She sighed. "You just don't have a business sense, Lila."

Lila shrugged. "I guess not. But then, I don't need one, do I?"

Fingering her earrings, Amy remarked, "You think Jessica will still talk to us little people when she's rich and famous?"

"Sure." Jessica grinned at her friends. "But first you'll have to make an appointment with my assistant."

"Oh, please," Cara said, laughing.

"Seriously, though, I have an idea," Jessica went on. She looked at Elizabeth, Olivia, and Enid. "This goes for you guys, too. You want to help me make some of the jewelry? It's really easy. I figure I'll put all the stuff in the basement, and—"

"In the basement?" Elizabeth said. "How much did you order?"

"Well," Jessica said, "just a few cartons."

"Really? Why so many?"

"Liz, *everyone* knows that if you order volume, you save money."

Elizabeth nodded. "Right, Jess."

But you had to pay for them somehow, she wanted to say. That discussion would have to wait until later, when she wouldn't be putting her sister on the spot.

Just then Jessica looked up abruptly. A big smile crossed her face as she leaped up from her seat. "Ronnie!" she exclaimed.

Elizabeth turned to see Ronnie rushing toward them, his hair hanging in strands across his forehead. She did a double take when she saw the expression on his face. The old cockiness was gone. Instead, his eyes were hollow and fearful, and he was looking straight at Elizabeth.

"Elizabeth!" he called out breathlessly. "I have to—"

But Jessica was already standing in front of Elizabeth, reaching for Ronnie's arm. "I need to talk to you about something," she said with a coy smile.

"Are *you* Elizabeth?" he replied, confused.

"No, I'm Jessica, but that's an easy mistake to—"

He practically pushed her aside to get to Elizabeth. "Where's Jeff?" he demanded. He didn't even seem to see Enid.

"He's taking a chemistry exam," Elizabeth said.

"An exam? During lunch?"

Elizabeth smiled. "It's a long story."

"Tell me the long story!"

"Sure, Ronnie," Elizabeth said, a little shaken by his intensity. "Well, five guys on the soccer team are in the same chem class. Tony Esteban managed to convince Mr. Russo that the soccer team would be nervous and distracted taking a test last period. Mr. Russo's such a big soccer fan, he said he'd let them all take the test earlier in the day."

"What's the room number?" Ronnie asked.

"Well, I'll be meeting Jeffrey outside in the hallway after lunch—"

"Just tell me the room number, OK, Elizabeth?"

Elizabeth shifted in her seat. "Ronnie, you can't interrupt him in the middle of a—"

"Never mind!" Ronnie said. "I'll find it myself."

With that, he spun away from her and ran out the door.

"Wait!" Elizabeth and Jessica shouted at the same time. But it was too late. They both sat back down, scowling.

"What's with him?" Enid asked.

"I don't know," Elizabeth said. "He makes me so mad! He's been hanging around Jeffrey all the time, like they've been best friends for years. I can't believe he thinks he can just barge in while Jeffrey's taking an exam!"

"I wouldn't get so excited about it, Liz. He

80

wouldn't do something that dumb. He probably just wants to wait around for him outside the room."

"Then why won't he wait here? It'll only be a few more minutes!"

Enid laughed. "Come on, Liz, Jeffrey can take care of himself. He'll deal with Ronnie."

"I don't know, Enid. He's been acting so strange ever since Ronnie started hanging around."

"He's got a lot on his mind, Liz—the game, the chemistry test—you've been saying so yourself!"

"I guess," Elizabeth said, turning her attention back to her lunch. But she knew that wasn't the whole answer. *Ronnie wants something from Jeffrey*, she said to herself. *And I'm going to find out what it is.*

Eight

Jeffrey could hear the minute hand clicking on the chemistry room clock. He rubbed his eyes and stared at the next question on the exam. *Molarity* vs. *molality*. He was sure he knew the difference, if only he could stop being so nervous. Jeffrey forced himself to concentrate on getting the answer right.

The next time he looked at the clock, there were ten minutes to go, and he had only three questions left. If he could get some partial credit on them, he might actually do pretty well. At least he'd have a shot at something above a C, which is what he needed to play on the soccer team next year. He could feel the adrenaline starting to course through his body, just as it did in a soccer game when he psyched himself up.

Then Jeffrey heard voices. Mr. Russo had wandered briefly into the hallway, and now he was talking to someone—no, arguing, it seemed.

Jeffrey looked back at his exam. Mr. Russo was raising his voice. The other person sounded upset. He was telling Mr. Russo he needed to see—

It's Ronnie, Jeffrey realized, sitting bolt upright. He looked over at the doorway. Mr. Russo was actually standing in it now, blocking Ronnie's entry.

"Look, you can get suspended for this," Mr. Russo said. "There's a test going on!"

"I know, I know," Ronnie answered. "Just let me talk to Jeff for a minute. It's really important!"

The four other soccer players in the room all looked up in surprise. *What is going on here?* Jeffrey wondered. He felt his face turning beet red.

"Listen, Ronnie," Mr. Russo said in a firm, angry voice, "I'm going to give you a chance to stand here like a considerate human being and wait ten minutes until the test is over. If you so much as say one more word or move one inch closer to me, I swear I will suspend you so fast, your head will spin. Understood?"

"Whoa! All right, Mr. Russo!" Tony Esteban blurted.

A cheer went up from the room. Mr. Russo turned back inside. "I can't believe you're all doing *so* well on this test that you don't need to pay attention anymore," he said.

The room became silent again as everyone returned to the exam. Out of the corner of his eye, Jeffrey could see Ronnie hovering outside the door.

When Jeffrey tried to focus on his paper, he couldn't remember any answers. Whatever concentration he'd had was now totally shot.

He struggled to concentrate on the second-to-last question, and before long he was scribbling away frantically, trying to make up for lost time. When the bell rang, signaling the end of lunch period, all five students in the room groaned, Jeffrey included.

"Come on, now, that wasn't so bad, was it?" Mr. Russo asked.

"Nah," Michael Schmidt said. "Piece of cake."

"Big talk, coming from the guy who thought uranium was the name of a planet," Tony retorted.

Laughter rang out as Michael gave Tony a playful punch in the shoulder.

But Jeffrey wasn't laughing. In fact, he was torn between two urges. The first one was to beg to take the exam again. The second was to tear Ronnie apart.

"Come on, French," Tony said. "If the inspiration hasn't hit by now . . ."

"Yeah, right," Jeffrey mumbled. Reluctantly

84

he picked up his exam and walked to the front of the room.

"Sorry about that, Jeffrey," Mr. Russo said. "I just couldn't let him in. I hope there's nothing wrong."

"I'm sure everything's OK," Jeffrey replied with a wan smile. He put the test on the desk and walked out.

As he got closer to Ronnie, Jeffrey felt rage building up inside him. He wanted to walk right past him, not even acknowledge him—or at least send off a signal so strong that even Ronnie would understand that he wanted him to get lost.

No such luck. Ronnie ran over to his side like an eager puppy. "Hi, Jeff!" he said. "How did it go?"

"It's *Jeffrey*," Jeffrey snapped. "No one calls me Jeff."

"Oh, sorry! Why didn't you tell me that before?"

Jeffrey spun around. "Look, Ronnie. There's plenty I haven't told you. Like the fact that even though I barely know you, you've become a total pain in the neck."

Ronnie stared backed at him, his eyes full of shock.

"I'm a very patient guy, Ronnie, but you've pushed me over the edge," Jeffrey went on, unable to stop himself. "What was that scene all about just now?"

"I—I need your help."

Jeffrey shook his head. "No. I know what you want. You want me to 'just lay back a little on Saturday,' right? You want me to make sure that *I* save you from the trouble *you* got yourself into!"

"Shh!" Ronnie said, looking nervously up and down the crowded hallway. "Can't we talk in a quieter place?"

"No, we can't. I don't know about you, but I have to get to class." Jeffrey started to walk down the hall away from him.

"Jeffrey!" Ronnie's voice rang out. It was so loud that everyone else in the hallway turned around. "Just talk to me a minute, OK?"

Tony, who was talking to a red-haired girl, called out, "Hey, French, why don't you see what the guy wants before he goes out of his mind?"

Jeffrey stood still for a moment. *Why should I even think of putting up with him?* he thought. *All he's going to do is tell me another lame story about Big Al and his threats.*

He glanced over his shoulder. Jeffrey wasn't sure, but he thought he could see Ronnie's knees shaking. Then his eyes caught sight of something he hadn't expected.

There was *sand* on Ronnie's shoes.

Jeffrey looked up. He'd been too angry to notice the haggard look on Ronnie's face, and the dark, wet stains on his clothing. *Maybe he really is in trouble*, he thought.

"Just for a second," Ronnie repeated.

With a sigh of resignation, Jeffrey said, "Sure."

Ronnie quickly led him to a secluded area at the end of a row of lockers. "You've got to help me, Jeffrey," he said in a hushed voice.

"Well, to tell you the truth, Ronnie, I've been thinking about what you told me." Jeffrey shook his head firmly. "It's just not going to work. You'll have to talk to this Big Al guy—"

"I *did* talk to him," Ronnie said desperately. "Jeffrey, it's even worse than I expected. He's starting *now*!"

"Starting what?"

"To harass me! I don't know if you noticed, but I wasn't in school this morning. I was at the beach, being a punching bag for one of Big Al's goons!"

Jeffrey's eyes grew wider. "What did he do to you?"

"Oh, nothing much." Ronnie gave a sarcastic little laugh. "Just pummeled me in the gut, smacked me up against a wooden pillar, and tossed me into a patch of wet sand. It was fun."

"I don't believe it! That guy really does mean business."

"That's what I've been trying to tell you all along. Now do you see why I need your help?"

Jeffrey couldn't answer right away. A strong voice inside him told him he could never *think* of doing anything underhanded in Saturday's game. The most important thing was playing to win. Anything less would be letting his teammates down.

But now he found himself staring at someone in trouble, someone who was hanging on to the hope that he would help get him out of it. How could he put the outcome of a game above something like that?

He felt his resolve weakening. "I don't know, Ronnie."

"Jeffrey, do you think I *like* to beg you like this? Don't you think I know what kind of pressure it puts on you? Normally I'd *never* ask something like this from anyone. But this isn't a normal situation." His pleading bloodshot eyes stared right into Jeffrey's. "Look, I know how much playing all out means to you, but I also know that last week, in back of the Dairi Burger, you helped out a total stranger. Now that total stranger is a friend, Jeffrey, a friend who needs you."

Jeffrey looked at the floor, still not sure what he should do.

"Look," Ronnie said, "if Big Mesa wins tomorrow, we all lose. But you and I both know that the Gladiators are going to win. Maybe you'll win by two points naturally, and you won't have to do anything." He shrugged. "But maybe not. Now, I don't know what'll happen to me if I don't deliver on this promise I made, but I know it'll be bad. I found that out today, the hard way. If you really do care about a friend, Jeffrey—if you really believe that saving someone's life is more important than a high-school soccer game—then you'll do this small favor for me."

The bell for the next period clanged through the now-empty hallway. Jeffrey was late for his next class, but he wasn't even thinking about that. Thoughts and images crowded his mind: a scoreboard that read Gladiators 3, Bulldogs 1; a wide-open net; the ball at his feet; a split-second shiver of excitement . . . contrasted with a look of utter terror on Ronnie's face.

Jeffrey could feel his skin crawling as he looked at Ronnie and nodded. "All right. I'll do it."

Nine

Jessica was out the classroom door even before the final bell had stopped ringing. She had found out from Bruce Patman that Ronnie's last class was math, in room 302, at the other end of the school.

She raced down the hallway, slipping through groups of students who were rushing to get home to start the weekend. She was still upset about not being able to talk to Ronnie during lunch, and she wasn't going to miss the opportunity now.

She ran around a corner and up to 302. A cluster of people stood outside the door, but Ronnie was nowhere in sight.

Peering inside, she saw him standing across the desk from his teacher, Mr. Frankel.

Jessica waited by the door. She couldn't help overhearing their conversation.

"Well, I'm sorry you don't want to talk about it, Ronnie," Mr. Frankel said. "But whatever the problem is, you know you can come in for extra tutoring. I'm just concerned about this sudden drop in your grades."

"OK, Mr. Frankel," Ronnie answered softly. "I'll come in for help next week."

"Good. In the meantime, try to get a little sleep. I hope you don't mind my saying this, but you've been looking pretty tired lately."

"Yeah, you're right, Mr. Frankel. Thanks. See you Monday."

It didn't exactly seem like the best time to approach Ronnie, but Jessica had no choice. If she wanted to start making jewelry over the weekend, she would have to get to the warehouse right after school, with the money.

She took a few steps back from the door and acted as if she just happened to be walking down the hallway. "Oh, hi, Ronnie!" she called out when he emerged from his classroom.

Ronnie looked up with a start. "Hi, Jessica," he said.

"Heading home?" she asked.

"No. I'm, uh, going to hang out for a while. I'm meeting someone later."

"Good. I have to stick around for cheerleading practice. I'll walk with you to your locker," Jessica said sweetly.

As the two of them started off down the

hallway, Jessica flashed Ronnie her most alluring smile, but he didn't seem to notice. "I have some good news for you," she said.

Ronnie's expression brightened a little. "What?"

"I decided to try to market my jewelry, and Treasure Island is going to carry it!"

"Great," Ronnie said, his faint smile fading fast.

"As a matter of fact, they said they'd take as many pieces as I could make."

"Uh-huh."

"So I've been doing a lot of phone calling to try to get materials together. You wouldn't believe how expensive some of the stuff is. Much more than I could hope to pay for myself." She gave a loud sigh. "Which is too bad, because if I can't raise the money for enough pieces, it just won't be worth it, and I'll have to give up the whole thing."

"Oh."

Come on, Ronnie! she thought. *Isn't that plain enough? Do I have to hit you over the head with it?*

Judging from the distracted look on his face, maybe she did.

"Wait a minute," she continued. "I just thought of something. Remember that day you came into the cafeteria with Jeffrey, and Cara was wearing my earrings?"

"I think so . . ." Ronnie murmured.

Jessica put her finger to her lips as if she were

trying to think of the incident. "I don't know if I remember this right, but didn't you mention something about putting up a thousand dollars or so?"

Ronnie looked at her blankly. "A thousand dollars?"

"Yes, that was it! I remember it now!" she said excitedly. "You said you'd be able to back me if I decided to sell my jewelry." Then she laughed and turned away. "Oh, listen to me! I'm sorry, Ronnie. I'm sure you were just kidding around."

Ronnie stopped walking and looked Jessica in the eye. "Jessica," he said, "I don't have a thousand dollars. At this point I don't even have a hundred dollars. And if I did, there's someone else I'd have to give it to."

Jessica glared at him. "But you *promised*—"

"Look, I don't remember what I said. But if you're expecting money from *me*"—he snorted and held his palms up to the sky—"forget it."

Jessica watched openmouthed as Ronnie shuffled off. She felt frozen to the floor. A minute ago there had been a whole new career ahead of her. Now she felt as if it had been plucked out of her hands.

Don't panic, she told herself. Forcing a smile, she began walking back up the hallway toward the gym. *You'll think of something.*

* * *

Elizabeth couldn't help worrying as she walked toward the *Oracle* office after school. She had gone to Jeffrey's chemistry class near the end of lunch period and had seen Ronnie pacing outside. Later on, Jeffrey had told her what had happened, and she still couldn't believe it.

As usual, the first thing Elizabeth heard when she entered the office was the voice of Penny Ayala, the newspaper's editor in chief. "Liz, we're going to need some space from you for spillover from the sports page."

Across the crowded newspaper office Penny was huddled over a mock-up of the newspaper with John Pfeifer, the sports editor.

"It's an incredible sports page," John said with a radiant grin. "Bound to rake in the prizes at this year's California high-school journalism competition. I'm running a feature on Coach Horner, and there's a play-by-play of last week's soccer game, and a big prechampionship preview. . . ." He shrugged. "But the problem is, I'm going to need more space for all of it."

"I think we can work with it if you keep 'Eyes and Ears' under ten column inches," Penny said. "Can you?"

"Sure," Elizabeth answered. "There isn't much gossip this week anyway." *At least nothing I would want to print*, Elizabeth said to herself, thinking of Ronnie. "And besides, it's for a good cause, isn't it?" she added, smiling.

"Yes," John told her. "You can be sure there'll be a nice long description of last week's winning goal." He began intoning in a melodramatic radio-announcer voice: "Never before in the history of Sweet Valley sports has a last-minute goal so captured the imaginations of the home crowd . . ."

Elizabeth rolled her eyes. "Please, spare me the dramatics. What's gotten into you today, anyway?"

Penny shielded her mouth from John with her hand. With a knowing smile, she mouthed, "He's in love."

"I saw that!" John said. "Spreading rumors about me again, are you?"

"Get to work," Penny said with a laugh.

"Yes, boss." Turning to Elizabeth, he said, "Listen, why don't you hurry up and finish your column? Then I'll walk over to soccer practice with you."

"OK," Elizabeth said. She looked forward to hanging out with one of Jeffrey's friends—one who wasn't named Ronnie.

"I'm home, Mom!" Jessica called out, shutting the front door behind her.

Immediately Prince Albert, the family's golden retriever, trotted into the room with a tennis ball in his mouth. He dropped the ball next to her and looked up expectantly, swinging his tail from side to side.

"Not now, Prince Albert," Jessica said.

As he wandered away, looking dejected, Mrs. Wakefield popped her head out of the kitchen. "Hi, honey! You just missed a call from Treasure Island. You're supposed to call them back as soon as possible."

"Uh-huh," Jessica said, then sighed forlornly as she walked into the kitchen.

Mrs. Wakefield looked at her quizzically. "I thought you'd be happy about that. Is something wrong?"

"Well . . . I think I need to talk to you about something, Mom."

"What is it, sweetheart?"

"Remember that two hundred dollars you said you'd lend me?"

"Oh, I almost forgot." Mrs. Wakefield reached for her purse, which was resting on a chair by the kitchen phone. "I took it out of the bank this afternoon. I knew you wanted to go to the—"

"No!" Jessica interrupted. "I—I don't think I'll be needing it after all." She cast her eyes downward.

Mrs. Wakefield put her hands on her hips. "After all that talk about profit margins and finding a market"—she raised an eyebrow—"and buying me my dream office?"

Jessica sighed dramatically again. "I know, Mom. But it's just that . . . well, I did some figuring and realized that it doesn't make much sense. I mean, in order to really go for it, two hundred dollars just isn't enough to make a good investment."

"Do I detect a subtle hint for more money?"

"No," Jessica replied. "I know the amount I want to spend would be too much. I had a long talk with the guy at the wholesale place, and I realized that what I needed would be way too much for me to ask for from you and Dad."

"How much is too much, Jessica?"

"Well . . . a *lot* more than two hundred," Jessica said.

"What? Four hundred? Five hundred?" her mother asked.

"I guess—something like that."

"You're right. That is too much."

Jessica drummed her fingers on the countertop. She had expected that reaction. "If only there were some easy way to borrow some money and pay back just a little at a time—you know, more when you're doing better, less when you're having a rough time."

"You mean like a credit card?"

Jessica's eyes lit up. "Mom, you're a genius! They have really low minimum payments, don't they?"

"Jessica," Alice Wakefield said, "I could see that one coming a mile away."

Jessica's heart sank.

"But I'll do it," Mrs. Wakefield said.

"You will?" Jessica looked at her mother's face closely, trying to see if she was serious.

"Yes, I will," Mrs. Wakefield said firmly. "You make jewelry, and when the bill comes in each month, you pay the monthly minimum." She took her credit card out of her purse and handed it to Jessica.

Jessica grabbed the card and wrapped her mother in a big hug. "Mom, you're the best!"

Mrs. Wakefield laughed. "Just take the card before I have second thoughts."

"OK! I think I'll go to the warehouse right now."

With that, Jessica raced out the front door. But as she climbed into the Fiat and started it up, she felt a small pang of guilt. How was she going to explain how much the stuff *really* cost?

Don't worry about it, a little voice inside her said. *By the time the bill comes in, you'll have made enough to pay the difference.*

But that meant selling a lot of jewelry. And she would only be able to sell a lot if she made a lot. Suddenly Jessica's elation was replaced by a feeling of gloom. Any hope of a fun, relaxing weekend had just gone up in smoke.

Ten

As John Pfeifer and Elizabeth approached the soccer field that afternoon, there were a dozen or so other people watching the practice—Winston Egbert, Bill Chase, DeeDee Gordon, and others. Off to the left, where the school's parking lot met the south end of the field, a heavy-set man was leaning against a long silver sedan, smoking a cigar. He was probably one of the players' fathers, Elizabeth thought. He was waving the cigar in the air and talking to someone. She couldn't tell who the other person was, because the heavy man was in the way.

Just beyond the onlookers a cloud of dust rose as a loud whistle blew. "Out of bounds, junior varsity!" Coach Horner's voice boomed out.

As Elizabeth got closer to the field, DeeDee turned around. "Hey, guys, hurry up! This is getting exciting!"

99

"What's going on?" Elizabeth asked.

"It's a tie, and the junior varsity team just stole the ball! They look great!"

Elizabeth frowned. That sounded strange; traditionally, the varsity rolled over the younger guys in practice.

She and John found a spot by the fence. There, Elizabeth caught a glimpse of Jeffrey pacing around in the center of the field, a dejected look on his face.

Just then the ball was thrown toward him from the sidelines. Aaron Dallas raced toward the goal at top speed. It was a play Elizabeth saw every week. Jeffrey would get the ball and kick it to a precise spot in front of the net. Aaron would arrive there the exact second the ball landed, and he'd boot it in. It was an exciting play, and most of the time it worked.

The inbounds pass blazed toward Jeffrey's ankle. As always, Jeffrey raised his foot to trap it. Aaron was now in full stride, looking over his shoulder for the pass.

But when Jeffrey put his foot down, he missed the ball, and it went skittering past him toward the middle of the field. A look of surprise flashed across his face, and he turned to run after the ball.

"Oh, come *on!*" John moaned. "That was definitely not vintage French."

Elizabeth winced as the JV halfback intercepted

the ball and kicked a perfect line drive into the varsity team's net. "Goal—junior varsity!" Coach Horner shouted through a bullhorn.

As play stopped, John shook his head and gave Elizabeth a questioning look. "You think there's too much pressure on him or something?" he asked.

Elizabeth laughed. "Oh, come on, John. It's only practice!" She ignored a voice inside her that said she had never seen Jeffrey fumble that play before.

"True." John rested his elbows on the fence. "But I tell you, I'd be nervous if I were in his shoes—with a championship game at stake, knowing that some guy in the stands is going to be taking note of my every move."

"Don't flatter yourself," Elizabeth said with a sly grin. "Jeffrey's not fazed by reporters."

John looked blank for a moment. Then he laughed. "No, not me. I'm talking about the scout!"

"What scout?"

John rolled his eyes. "You didn't know? Some big honcho from Branford College is coming to the game."

Elizabeth's eyes widened. "Are you serious? They're one of the big soccer powers on the West Coast. Jeffrey's *always* talking about their team."

"Well, their best halfbacks are graduating next

year, and apparently the coach is interested in Jeffrey."

"That's fantastic!" Elizabeth said. "I wonder why he didn't tell me."

John shrugged. "Maybe he doesn't know. I just found out after school when I ran into the team manager. I assumed everyone knew about it, but I might be wrong."

Elizabeth looked back out onto the field. She hoped John was right. Jeffrey would never keep something like that from her, unless their differences lately had been more serious than she thought.

Out on the field, she saw Jeffrey kick a stone in frustration. Hoping he'd look her way, Elizabeth gave a little wave. But Jeffrey didn't seem to notice. His eyes were darting over to the parking lot.

Both John and Elizabeth followed his gaze.

"Well, what do you know?" John said. "We have a surprise visitor."

"Who?" Elizabeth asked.

John pointed to the heavyset man by the silver car. "That's Al Remsen. He's a spotter for some big-time L.A. bookies—a real slimeball from everything I've heard. He stakes out college and high-school games."

"What's he doing here?" Elizabeth said.

"Beats me. Sweet Valley is a cinch to win this game. He's usually only interested in games with a closer point spread."

At that moment the man walked forward to lean on the fence, and the person beside him, who had been hidden, was now clearly visible.

Ronnie Edwards.

John shrugged. "He also likes games he can fix." He chuckled as if to show how silly that remark was.

Elizabeth smiled back at him, but she felt a shiver run down her back.

After practice Elizabeth waited patiently outside the back of the school for Jeffrey. He was usually one of the first players out of the locker room, but that afternoon he was a little late.

Elizabeth kept her eyes on the scene at the edge of the parking lot while she waited. The man who John had identified as Al Remsen was sitting calmly in the front seat of his sedan, blowing rings of cigar smoke out the window. The smoke was enveloping Ronnie's face, but he seemed oblivious. He was gesturing nervously with his arms while he jabbered away about something.

But it was more than just jabbering, Elizabeth noticed. His face had a tight, defensive look. It looked more like he was pleading.

Before long, Remsen rolled up his blue-tinted window, and the car roared away. Elizabeth averted her eyes as Ronnie shuffled dejectedly toward his Mustang, parked at the other end of the lot.

Just then, Jeffrey appeared in the doorway. "Hi, Liz!" he said, beaming at her.

Elizabeth loved the way Jeffrey looked right after practice, with his hair still slicked back from the shower. "Hi! That was some scrimmage."

Jeffrey grimaced. "Yeah. That's the best the B team ever played. For a while I thought they were going to beat us."

"I didn't," Elizabeth said confidently. "I knew you guys would win." All of a sudden she couldn't imagine what she and Jeffrey had been disagreeing about.

Grateful to finally have some quiet, private time with her boyfriend, she linked her arm in his as they walked toward the front of the school, where his car was parked.

"Listen, I'm really sorry I didn't meet you after the chem exam, Liz," Jeffrey said. "It's just that when Ronnie decides he wants to talk, he has to. He's—kind of confused these days."

"Is anything wrong with him?" Elizabeth asked.

Jeffrey opened the passenger door of his car for Elizabeth. "He's having a few personal problems. I guess I've become some sort of brother figure to him."

Elizabeth nodded and climbed in. Jeffrey got

into the driver's seat and started the car without saying another word.

As Jeffrey pulled away from the curb, Elizabeth let out a loud sigh. "Jeffrey, can we talk?"

"Isn't that what we're doing?" Jeffrey smiled.

"No, I mean *really* talk. About Ronnie."

She watched Jeffrey's face carefully. There wasn't much of a change—only a tiny flicker of worry in his eyes—but it was enough to make her tense up inside. Something was definitely wrong.

"What do you mean, Liz?"

"Well, I was wondering about his, uh, *personal* problem. Does it have anything to do with someone named Al Remsen, by any chance?"

Jeffrey's face lost a lot of its postpractice color. "Al Remsen?" he asked.

"He's a gambler from L.A. John Pfeifer noticed him watching the scrimmage with Ronnie from the parking lot."

For a few moments Jeffrey silently stared at the road. Finally, as he stopped for a red light, he sighed heavily and said, "You're right, Liz. It does have to do with Al Remsen. I'd never even heard of Remsen until recently, but Michael told me he saw him at the practice session today."

Elizabeth turned and looked at Jeffrey. "Is Ronnie in some sort of trouble?"

Jeffrey nodded. "You've got to promise to

keep this between you and me. I told Ronnie I wouldn't tell anybody."

"You know you can trust me, Jeffrey. I'm just worried about you—and us."

"I know," Jeffrey said sadly. He paused for a moment, as if he wanted to choose his next words carefully. "Ronnie got mixed up with this Remsen guy pretty seriously. He started placing a few small bets last year and collected on just about all of them. Remsen took a big cut, but Ronnie still made a lot of money. He was hooked. The bets got bigger and bigger until Ronnie started making a lot of money, and the more he made, the more credit Remsen gave him against his share. With each bet, Ronnie ran up an IOU. With the extra money, he could place even more bets. Then suddenly Remsen decided to collect, and Ronnie was in the hole for two thousand dollars."

"Two thousand!" Elizabeth gasped. "Does he have that much?"

"No, that's the problem. And when Ronnie said he couldn't pay, Remsen threatened him. They worked out an arrangement, but even so, Remsen sent someone to rough him up—just for fun, to remind him to keep the deal."

Elizabeth shivered. It all sounded so serious now. "What sort of arrangement, Jeffrey?"

"Hmm?"

"With Remsen. What kind of arrangement did Ronnie make?"

Jeffrey's shoulders slumped slightly. For a long moment he remained silent. Finally he said in a low voice, "He agreed to guarantee a point spread in Saturday's game."

"You mean fix the game, don't you?" Elizabeth inquired.

"Well, not exactly—"

"And how does Ronnie plan to do this?" Elizabeth cut him off angrily. "What do you have to do, Jeffrey?"

"Ronnie . . ." Jeffrey's voice trailed off. For the first time since Elizabeth had known him, Jeffrey looked like a frightened child. "Ronnie asked me to make sure Sweet Valley doesn't win by more than two points."

Elizabeth felt frozen with shock. So that was it—the reason Jeffrey had been so torn up, the reason Ronnie had been trailing after him so much. Now it all made sense.

She shook her head. "You told him no, right?"

Jeffrey didn't answer.

"Jeffrey, say something!"

"Well, at first I told him no. But he kept bugging me, and after he was beaten up at the beach, he told me his life was in danger. And it is!"

"So you're going to play badly on purpose, just because—"

"Just because *what*, Elizabeth?" Jeffrey snapped. Suddenly his eyes were ablaze with emotion.

107

"Just because Ronnie might be hurt or killed? I mean, come *on*. I know the game is important, but we're talking about the real world here! When guys like Al Remsen don't get their way, they hurt people. What am I supposed to do? Stick to my principles and let him do what he wants to Ronnie? That would really teach him a lesson, wouldn't it?" He looked away from the road and glared briefly at Elizabeth.

She folded her arms and looked straight ahead. His argument made sense, but somehow that didn't make it any better. She shook her head again in disbelief. "I just don't understand how you could even *think* of doing something like that, Jeffrey, betraying the team, taking Ronnie's responsibility on your shoulders—especially with that scout coming."

Jeffrey opened his mouth as if to interrupt her, but nothing come out. Instead, he gave her a baffled look. "Scout? What scout?"

"The scout from Branford College!" Elizabeth said. "I mean, he's coming to the game just to see you."

"Wait a minute. No one told me about this," Jeffrey protested. "Are you sure it's true?"

"Well, that's what John Pfeifer says. Supposedly Branford's star halfbacks are graduating a year from June—"

"That's right," Jeffrey said pensively. "I knew about that." A dazed smile crossed his face. "I would *love* to play for Branford. I never thought they'd consider me."

"You're the best, Jeffrey! That's why I can't understand what you're telling me. I mean, this is more than just a silly high-school game. And even if it weren't, what kind of friend would make you stoop so low? I'm sure there's got to be more than one way out."

Jeffrey's will seemed to be weakening. "I just don't know, Liz. This whole situation has become so confusing, and so frightening." Jeffrey shook his head. "I don't know what to do anymore."

"I'm sure we can think of another way to get Ronnie out of trouble," Elizabeth said. "One that won't put you on the line, too." *The question is,* Elizabeth thought to herself as she stared out the side window, *can we do it before game time?*

Eleven

Jessica held up the necklace she had just created. She couldn't help smiling from ear to ear. It was stunning—her best design by far. She laid the necklace carefully on a rectangle of white cotton in a small box and sat back. Heaving a sigh, she looked around the garage. It had been an incredible push, working late into Friday night and then getting Cara and Amy to help her the next morning. Now Cara and Amy were long gone—in fact, they had left at eleven, over an hour and a half ago.

Jessica felt a little strange having let her sister take the car to the game without her. The irony had been almost too much to bear—*Elizabeth* driving off to have fun, while *Jessica* stayed home to work. Jessica had had to fight the urge to run outside when she heard the car start up. But she'd already made her choice, and she had to stick with it. The jewelry came first.

And her choice had paid off. Finally the work was done—at least enough of it to make Jessica feel secure. If she was lucky she would sell the pieces in a month or two, and the credit card bill would be a thing of the past.

In a corner of the worktable, a number of small white jewelry boxes were piled high. Each one contained one of Jessica's creations. Quickly she put them all in a shopping bag and set them aside to take to Treasure Island. Lila was due to pick her up in a few minutes. If she came on time, they would get to the stadium with only a half hour to spare before the game.

Jessica rushed inside to get into her cheerleading outfit. As she flew through the kitchen she heard the phone ring. "Mom, can you get that?" she called out.

She ran into her room, slammed the door shut, and pulled her cheerleading outfit out of the closet.

"Jessica!" her mother's voice called out.

Jessica pulled her jersey down over her head and answered, "Who is it?"

For a split second Jessica froze, realizing she had forgotten to return the call from Treasure Island the day before. "Just a minute!"

She quickly stepped into her skirt, pulled it

up, grabbed her socks and sneakers, and ran into the kitchen.

Jessica almost blurted a breathless hello into the receiver. But at the last second, she held it away from her face and counted to three. Then, with a professional-sounding coolness, she said, "Yes? Jessica speaking."

"Hello, Jessica?" Ms. Lussier's voice said.

Cradling the receiver in her shoulder, Jessica perched on her right foot while pulling a sock over her left. "Yes, hello, Ms. Lussier. I'm *so* sorry I didn't return your call earlier, but I've been busy putting together my pieces for you."

"Oh, dear," Ms. Lussier said. "I hope you haven't gotten too far along."

Jessica shifted her weight to her left foot and began slipping the other sock on. *Maybe she's run out of storage space,* she thought. "Well, actually, I've got enough for a nice display. I could keep the rest at home if you don't have enough room."

"Well—perhaps you should hold on to them, sweetheart. They really are lovely, and I'm sure there are *so* many other shops that would be thrilled to take a chance on them."

Jessica almost fell over, but she caught herself at the last second. "I'm not sure I know what you mean, Ms. Lussier."

Ms. Lussier's long sigh made Jessica dread

her next words. "I must tell you, I'm very, very upset. The owner called me into a meeting yesterday. It seems that they want to change the store's image—concentrate more on shoes and upscale clothing. They feel it will help Treasure Island expand from a small Southern California chain into a more diverse national organization."

"So you won't be selling jewelry?" Jessica's voice was practically a whisper.

"No, we'll be selling jewelry, but on a much more limited basis. Unfortunately, that means cutting back on all but the most tried-and-true designers."

"But I'm sure my jewelry will outsell them! Why don't I just drop off what I have?" Jessica suggested.

There was a brief, tense silence, and Jessica felt her spirits sink. "I would love to—really I would," Ms. Lussier said. "But I'm afraid the decision is final."

"Uh-huh," Jessica mumbled. At this point the last thing on her mind was sounding cool and professional.

"I'm sorry, Jessica. I know I raised your hopes so high. This must be a disappointment to you."

Honnnk! The sound of Lila's horn startled Jessica. She checked her watch again. "Ms. Lussier," she said firmly, "I'll see you in about five minutes."

Without listening for an answer, Jessica hung up the phone. As she hastily pulled on her sneakers, she could think of only one thing: *Upscale clothing or not, my jewelry will be on that shelf before the game starts.*

Elizabeth drove the red Fiat slowly through the boisterous pregame crowd in the Sweet Valley High parking lot. It was already packed with cars. Wedged into the passenger seat, Enid and Hugh leaned forward, looking for a spot.

Seeing a space at the far end, Elizabeth carefully pulled in and shut off the car.

"If I'd known you were going to park this far away, I would have brought my hiking boots and some trail mix," Enid teased.

Elizabeth made a face. "You'd better watch it, or you won't get a ride home," she warned.

"It'll be tough, Enid, but I think you can make it," Hugh said with a laugh, opening the door. "Of course, if Big Mesa wins, *I'll* definitely have to walk." Hugh was a student at Big Mesa.

"I wouldn't worry about that," Elizabeth said, laughing. "They don't stand a chance."

The three of them got out of the car and continued bickering good-naturedly as they walked toward the stadium, alongside dozens of other Sweet Valley and Big Mesa students. Elizabeth could feel the energy in the air, but she couldn't get too excited about the game. She had thought about Jeffrey's problem for hours the night before, and she still had no idea how to solve it. She could only hope that Ronnie was bluffing and that Jeffrey would be able to play his best with a clear conscience.

To their left, Winston, Tom McKay and Bill Chase were holding a banner that read Phi Epsilon Says Go Gladiators! Winston caught Elizabeth's glance and shrugged. "OK, so it's not that original," he called out. "It wasn't *my* idea!"

Elizabeth couldn't help but giggle. Just then she spotted Julie and Johanna Porter ahead of them. She cupped her hand to her mouth to shout something to Julie but then stopped short.

Out of the corner of her eye she saw Ronnie's car creeping through the parking lot.

She turned to Enid and Hugh. "Listen, guys," she said, "I left my sunglasses in the car. You go on ahead. Save me a seat—on the Sweet Valley side, of course," she said teasingly to Hugh.

"We can wait," Enid suggested.

"No, go ahead. The longer we wait, the worse our seats will be."

"OK. See you in a minute."

Elizabeth walked back toward her Fiat, watching Ronnie's car as it pulled into a nearby spot.

She mentally reviewed the list of questions she wanted to ask him.

Looking over her shoulder to make sure Hugh and Enid were out of sight, she began walking straight toward Ronnie's car. Elizabeth noticed that Ronnie looked haggard and tense as he got out.

Instead of walking toward the stadium, he turned. Pulling up behind his car was a Lincoln Continental, exactly like the one Al Remsen had been driving the day before.

Elizabeth watched as a burly man in sunglasses hopped out and greeted Ronnie with a wide grin. He was bigger and younger-looking than Remsen and had a shock of jet-black hair.

She pulled back, but their brief conversation was still clearly audible.

"I—I told you everything was arranged," she heard Ronnie say.

"Fine," the other man replied in an overly polite voice. "Then how about you and me listening to the game together?"

With that, the man opened the door to his car and gestured for Ronnie to step inside. Meekly Ronnie followed his orders. The man then slammed the door shut and walked around to the driver's side, glowering.

Elizabeth sprinted toward the Fiat. When she hopped inside, she spotted the Continental working its way to the parking lot exit, its horn laring at the meandering crowd of students in ts way.

Following that car was Elizabeth's only chance to find out what was going on with Ronnie and Big Al, her only hope to help Jeffrey. Quickly she backed out of her parking space.

As she drove toward the exit, she suddenly realized that Ronnie had been telling Jeffrey the truth: His life certainly looked as if it were in danger.

Twelve

Jeffrey dribbled the ball downfield, going through his pregame practice routine. It was twenty minutes before game time, and already the stands were full. The stadium reverberated with an excited hum. Most of the cheerleaders had arrived, and they were going through drills on the sidelines.

But for all the activity around him, Jeffrey felt lifeless inside. The sight of his opponents warming up, the sound of the people in the stands, the smell of the fresh-cut grass—all of the things that usually made his blood race before a game—weren't affecting him at all.

"I don't know about you, but I am *fired up!*" Aaron said as Jeffrey ran past him. Aaron was bouncing up and down on his feet, taking deep breaths to release tension. He took a playful swipe at Jeffrey's ball, but Jeffrey tapped it out of his reach.

Jeffrey smiled as best he could. "Yeah, me, too," he answered, giving his best friend a quick high-five.

I only wish I were, Jeffrey thought. *Come on, Jeffrey,* he said to himself. *There's a scout in the stands—get psyched!* He tried as hard as he could to forget about Ronnie, to think only of the ball, the field, and the net. Twenty yards away from him, the net stood open. He pulled back his foot and let loose a hard shot.

A sharp *whack* resounded as the ball flew through the air and veered just to the left of the net.

Jeffrey felt his body go slack. If he could miss an empty net, he was too distracted even to play in the game, never mind win it.

Sighing, he realized that helping Ronnie might be easier than he thought. The way he was feeling, he might not even have to *try* to lay back.

"Way to go, French! Fool the other team into thinking we left our glasses home, then move in for the kill!"

Jeffrey looked over to see Tony Esteban grinning at him. He nodded, trying to look confident.

A free ball was lying at the base of the fence that separated the field from the stands. As Jeffrey trotted over to retrieve it, he glanced up into the seats. Near the center of the field he saw A.J. sitting with some of his friends. Below them, to the left, Enid and Hugh were sitting in front of Winston. All three were laughing as if one of them had just told a joke. Jeffrey looked for Elizabeth, but she was nowhere in sight.

Jeffrey had a hollow feeling in the pit of his stomach. At this point the sight of Elizabeth's reassuring smile was probably the only thing that would make him feel better.

His eyes scanned the entire Sweet Valley side of the stadium, and that's when he saw a vaguely familiar figure walking toward the stands. The man was chomping on a cigar, looking at the field through mirrored sunglasses.

Al Remsen.

Jeffrey tried to swallow the lump in his throat. He looked around for Ronnie, but there were so many people in the stands that he couldn't see him.

Coach Horner's whistle suddenly sounded, followed by a loud, enthusiastic, "Yeah!" from Michael Schmidt. Yelling loudly and slapping their palms together, Jeffrey's teammates started off the field toward the locker room for a last-minute pep talk.

Jeffrey followed them. His pulse was pounding, but not for the right reasons. In the locker room he glumly took a place on the bench as Coach Horner paced back and forth in front of them. "OK, you guys, we've waited a long time for this," he began.

"All *right!*" Aaron encouraged everyone.

As the coach went on, his eyes lit up with excitement. "We've got some good news and some bad news. The good news is that the weather service says the rainstorm has gone off to the ocean. It's going to be cool and slightly overcast, a perfect day for soccer."

A few excited whoops went up around Jeffrey.

"The bad news is that it looks like those rumors about Jack Everly were right. He's recovered enough to see limited action today. If things start getting out of hand for the Bulldogs—and we're going to make sure that happens—they'll probably put him in the game." The coach planted his hands on his hips and looked straight at his team. "Now, is that going to bother *us?*"

"*No!*"

"That's what I want to hear! Now, get out there. And the next time I come in here, I want to be looking at the division champs!"

At once every player rose to his feet and let out a cheer. A chant of "Coach! Coach! Coach!" rang out, and everyone joined in, including Jeffrey. Slowly the cloud of gloom he felt surrounding him began to clear. He was surrounded by his best friends, on the verge of the most important sports event of his life, with a scout from one of the country's best soccer schools in the stands. A sudden thought flashed through his mind, a thought so incredibly obvious, he couldn't ignore it: *Why fight what comes naturally?*

"Yeah, Coach!" he cried. He felt Aaron's hand slapping him on the back, and he reached out to grab him by the shoulders.

Then, out of the corner of his eye, he spotted the team manager, Dave Evans, trying to get his attention.

"Jeffrey," Dave said, holding out a telegram, "this is for you."

Aaron's face broke into a crinkled smile. "Who-o-oa!" he called out, loud enough for everyone else to hear. "Jeffrey's got an urgent missive! Could it *possibly* be from Elizabeth Wakefield?"

Jeffrey felt his face turn red as he took the telegram from Dave. All his teammates' eyes were focused on him. Trying to hold back an embarrassed grin, he folded up the note to read later.

"Open it!" Michael Schmidt yelled. Brad Tomasi echoed that remark, and another chant began.

"Open it! Open it! Open it!"

Jeffrey laughed and shook his head. "Thanks a lot, Aaron," he muttered. Reluctantly, he opened the envelope, pulled out the message, and glanced at it.

Suddenly he felt his jaw go slack. He closed up the telegram and forced a smile. "Elizabeth says good luck, guys!"

"All right!" Aaron shouted. "Let's get 'em!"

As his teammates stormed out of the locker

room, Jeffrey stayed behind for a second to read the telegram again. He couldn't believe what he'd seen the first time.

Sure enough, the words glared up at him:

FRENCH:
  IF YOU WANT TO SEE YOUR LITTLE PAL AGAIN, JUST MAKE SURE YOU DON'T PLAY YOUR BEST TODAY.

BIG AL

Elizabeth watched the silver Continental disappear around a corner two blocks ahead. It was hard to keep pace with it, yet stay far enough behind so it wouldn't be obvious she was tailing it.

She tried to memorize the route they had just taken, counting the blocks, remembering the turns. The only way she would be able to get out of the unfamiliar neighborhood would be to retrace her steps. Elizabeth gulped as she looked around her. It was a section of town she remembered seeing only once. Years ago she had been there with her father on a trip to the municipal dump, which had since been closed down. In fact, it seemed that just about everything had been closed down. Faded signs peered down from old, abandoned factory buildings.

But as the Continental drove farther into the neighborhood, the buildings became sparser.

On both sides, vacant, weed-covered lots stretched back from the sidewalk.

Suddenly Elizabeth braked. Just ahead of her, the Continental had pulled into one of the lots.

Elizabeth glided slowly into a parking lot next to a nearby warehouse, where her car would be shielded from view. After hopping out, she gently closed the door and peeked around the side of the warehouse.

The Continental was parked next to a dingy one-story stucco building. Above the front door a rusted metal sign hung lopsided—Wilby's Bar & Grill. Venetian blinds had been drawn shut inside the front and side windows.

Elizabeth felt as if her throat were coated with cotton. The slight pinging of the Fiat's engine as it cooled down sounded to her like the clanging of a hammer. Every muscle in her body tensed. She angled herself so that she would be able to sprint to her car at a moment's notice.

Just then the driver's door of the Continental swung open. Quickly the dark-haired man got out of the car, yanked Ronnie out of the backseat, and pushed him into the building.

Elizabeth knew she had to do something. She looked left and right, but there were no other cars in sight, no other people. Crouching low to the ground, Elizabeth sneaked up to the side of the building and huddled underneath one of the windows. Inside, she could hear Ronnie's terrified voice.

"Wh-where are we? Why did you bring me here?"

Slowly she raised her head to look over the edge of the windowsill. The slats of the venetian blinds were separated just enough for her to catch a narrow glimpse of the room inside.

A dusty wooden bar stretched along the right-hand wall at the opposite end. A few empty bottles lay on top of it, reflected in the cracked mirror behind them. Next to the bottles was a shiny new portable radio.

At first Elizabeth couldn't see anybody, but then Ronnie popped into sight, backing away to the opposite wall near the bar. "Come on, Max," he said, cowering with fright. "You don't have to do that, do you?"

Max's cold, raspy voice sent a shiver up Elizabeth's spine. "Just following orders, kid," he said. "Relax."

Slowly he came into view. The sickeningly sweet grin was on his face again as he held something up for Ronnie to see.

Elizabeth stifled a gasp. Dangling from Max's right hand was a long rope tied in a hangman's noose!

For a moment Elizabeth couldn't move. If she screamed, no one would hear her. If she went inside to try to save Ronnie, Max would take her captive.

I've got to call the police! she realized. As she backed away from the window, she looked around for a phone booth. There wasn't one in sight. Elizabeth ran around to the back of the building, wincing as her feet noisily hit the gravel.

She found an abandoned gas station on the other side of the building, and there, on the wall, was an old, rusty phone booth.

Elizabeth sprinted up to it and picked up the receiver. Her heart jumped when she heard a faint dial tone. She struggled to keep her fingers steady as she dialed 911.

"Emergency," a voice at the other end answered.

"Hello, I'm—"

But those were the only words she could get out before a large hand clamped over her mouth.

"Aughh—"

A choked scream was all Elizabeth could manage as she felt herself being dragged backward toward the building.

Thirteen

"And now for the home team!" a voice blared over the stadium loudspeakers. "The Sweet Valley Gladiators!"

Jeffrey's cleats pounded the earth as he ran onto the field. Around him, students were on their feet, stomping rhythmically, throwing their fists in the air, yelling out the names of their favorite players.

Jeffrey could feel his blood pumping, but it wasn't because of the crowd noise. It was because of the telegram. Big Al's cold threat was imprinted on his mind. Ronnie's life actually depended on the outcome of this game.

His eyes searched the stands for Elizabeth, hoping the sight of her would calm him down, make him think clearer. Immediately his eye was caught by a man scribbling on a yellow pad just behind the Sweet Valley bench. He was wear a baseball cap with the word *Branford* sewn onto the visor.

It was the scout, and for all Jeffrey knew, he was taking notes about him right now.

A few rows behind the scout, Al Remsen sat impassively puffing a cigar, alone. Hugh and Enid were setting in the same spot as before, still talking to Winston. Where was Ronnie? Jeffrey wondered. And where was Elizabeth? It wasn't like her to be late to a game, especially for such an important one.

Jeffrey felt more confused by the minute.

"Get your hands off me!" Elizabeth scratched and kicked the man as he dragged her into the cavernous, deserted bar.

"Look who I found making a phone call outside," he said, glaring at Ronnie. "This a friend of yours?"

"Elizabeth!" Ronnie cried out, still standing against the far wall of the bar. Then, in a quavering voice, he added, "L-let go of her, Max."

The man grabbed a wooden chair from behind Elizabeth and pushed her onto it, keeping a tight painful grip on her arm. The rope that he had been holding was now slung over his shoulder.

Max snickered. "You're really sending the tough ones after me, aren't you?" With his free hand, he held the noose near Elizabeth's face. "Sweetheart, you've come to the wrong place."

Elizabeth's body stiffened with panic, but she tried to sit as calmly as possible. She had been in enough dangerous situations to know that showing fear was the worst thing she could do.

Besides, the hangman's noose had to be a scare tactic. He couldn't be serious—or could he? Was Ronnie in *that* much trouble?

Max's cheek muscles tightened slightly. He lowered the noose. Obviously he wasn't going to hang anybody, but he seemed angry that Elizabeth hadn't melted with fright from his threat.

"Brave, aren't you?" Max said.

Elizabeth stared back silently, trying to think of a way to escape.

"The quiet ones are the worst," he muttered. Then, with precise, mechanical motions, he slung the rope around Elizabeth and began tying her to the chair.

"Leave her alone!" Ronnie pleaded.

"I don't trust her," Max said. After tying a knot in the rope, he pulled a handkerchief from his coat pocket. "All I need is for someone to drive by and hear a shriek."

Elizabeth spluttered helplessly as he tied the handkerchief around her mouth.

"Now," Max said, stepping back, "we're all going to wait here nice and quiet until the soccer game is over, right?" He shot Ronnie a look over his shoulder. "Don't think I've forgotten about you, kid. I've got another rope."

He walked over to the bar, flicked on the radio that sat next to the old bottles, then leaned over the bar and reached into the shelves behind it.

The room echoed with the sound of the radio announcer's voice:

"... KSVH, the radio station of Sweet Valley. The big news here at Sweet Valley Stadium is the health of Jack Everly, Big Mesa's star halfback. Contrary to what his doctors have been saying all week, it appears he may see some action in this game."

"Your friend's gonna have a tough job," Max said, pulling out another rope from behind the bar.

Ronnie's eyes darted from Max to Elizabeth. His Adam's apple bobbed up and down, and he nodded wanly.

"... ball is intercepted by Jeffrey French of the Gladiators! He runs down the field ... and loses the ball! But it's picked up by Schmidt, who looks for an opening. He passes to Dallas—SCORE!"

Elizabeth's heart sank. Jeffrey hardly ever lost control of the ball. Maybe Ronnie had gotten through to him. Maybe Jeffrey *was* trying to fix the game!

"He better try harder than that," Max said. "Because Big Al has some plans if he doesn't. Not only for you, but for French, too."

Elizabeth swallowed nervously. Jeffrey was in trouble, and he didn't even know it! She had to do something. With a burst of energy, she swung her head left and right, attempting to loosen the handkerchief around her mouth.

But before she could say anything, Max ran over to her. "I knew this thing was going to be too small," he said. "What are you squirming for, kid? You might as well relax. It's gonna be a long game."

As he reached for the handkerchief, Elizabeth pulled her head back away from him. "Wait!" she said, her voice muffled by the cloth. "Just tell me what's going to happen to Jeffrey French."

Max grinned evilly. "The same thing that happens to your friend Ronnie—whatever that is."

Elizabeth's eyes flashed toward Ronnie, but he wasn't in the same spot. Slowly, tentatively, he was inching his way toward Max. When Elizabeth saw him, he waved his hand, signaling her to ignore him.

Max rubbed his chin, obviously happy to have broken through Elizabeth's cool exterior. "I haven't really decided yet. I could just knock out a few teeth, break their kneecaps. Or maybe I'll do something a little more fun, like tying them back-to-back and leaving them in the basement here. There's a nice family down there who'd like to meet them—a family of rats!"

Max snorted with laughter at his own joke.

Ronnie was now directly behind Max, a look of blind panic on his face.

"You're—you're a monster!" Elizabeth shouted. She lurched around in her chair, purposely trying to keep Max's attention away from Ronnie.

Ronnie reached out and grabbed a large bottle from the bar. His fingers were shaking with fear.

"A monster! Hey, that's not very nice," Max taunted. "I think your friend needs a lesson in manners, Edwards. What do you think?" he asked, spinning around to look at Ronnie. "Hey! What the—"

Elizabeth cringed at the sound of shattering glass as Ronnie hit Max in the head. The man's body went limp, and he fell to the floor in a heap.

Elizabeth looked up to see Ronnie, wide-eyed with shock, holding the neck of a broken liquor bottle in his right hand.

Fourteen

"There's one!" Ronnie shouted.

Elizabeth braked to a stop across the street from a phone booth. Her memory had served her better than she thought it would, and she had been able to get back into town with only one or two wrong turns. They had decided to get away from Max first, in case he woke up, and then call the police.

She reached for the door handle, but Ronnie put out his hand to stop her. "I'll do it," he said. "This'll give me more pleasure than you can know."

Elizabeth waited patiently while Ronnie ran over to the phone to make the call. He was back in what seemed like only a few seconds.

"What did you tell them?" Elizabeth asked as she pulled away from the curb.

"The whole thing. What happened this afternoon, where to find Max—and where to find Big Al."

"You must have talked fast."

Ronnie grinned. "Good news is hard to tell slowly."

As they drove across town toward the stadium, Ronnie turned on the car radio. A static-like noise crackled over the air. But Elizabeth could tell it wasn't static; it was cheering.

"*. . . and the Big Mesa crowd is on its feet!*" the announcer's voice cried out over the din. "*That's the second goal in the last minute and a half, and the Sweet Valley team is looking ragged and disappointed. So as we approach the end of the first quarter, the score is Big Mesa two, Sweet Valley one!*"

"Oh, no," Ronnie muttered.

Elizabeth knew she had to get to Jeffrey right away. Between quarters would be a perfect time. She would be able to call him over from the sidelines and tell him what had just happened, so that he'd know that the police were onto Big Al and that he could relax and play his best.

But would it do any good at this point? she wondered. Even if Jeffrey knew that Ronnie was all right, he was probably still too frazzled by the things that had been happening all week to play well. It might just be too late for him to get his concentration back. By now the Branford scout was probably wondering why he had even bothered coming to look at Jeffrey—if he hadn't left already!

She gripped the steering wheel and stared straight ahead. She wanted to say something to Ronnie, but she didn't know where to begin. Should she yell at him for getting Jeffrey into this mess, or thank him for saving her life?

Ronnie lowered his head and spoke up first. "Elizabeth, I—I'm so sorry about everything. I hope you know that. It's all my fault, and I'm sorry."

"Ronnie, I know I should be grateful to you for being so brave back there. You were great! But there's so much I don't understand." She shook her head with exasperation. "Why did you get involved in all this?"

"I don't know . . . At the beginning it all seemed like a game. And I was so good at it. I couldn't believe how easy it was to make money. Anyway, I was only going to do it for a little while, just long enough to get my father and me out of our rut. I guess I got too greedy."

"Ronnie, guys like Al Remsen don't think of gambling as a game," Elizabeth said.

"I know. But I always figured if anything bad happened, I'd be able to take care of it myself. I never thought I'd have to drag anyone else into this." He sighed. "You know, Elizabeth, if I had one wish in life, it would be to go back to the first time I ever met Big Al and just walk away from him."

"Well, we have to figure out what to do *now*,

Ronnie. There's an important college scout in the audience to see Jeffrey."

Ronnie shook his head. "Great. And there he is, trying to fix the score of the game, and it's all because of me."

"You know what, Ronnie?" Elizabeth said. "I want Sweet Valley to win more than anything else, but I would rather see them lose this game than win by two points."

Ronnie didn't answer. He just kept looking down at the floor of the car. "I know," he said softly. "I don't blame you."

Before long Elizabeth could see banners rising over a set of tall bleachers at the stadium. The noise of the crowd swelled just as Elizabeth pulled into the parking lot.

Every space in the lot was full, but Elizabeth had no intention of looking around for a free spot. She drove right up beside the bleachers and set the emergency brake.

"And as we begin the second quarter," the radio announcer said, *"the score is still Big Mesa two, Sweet Valley one. If the Bulldogs can hold on, it'll be a major upset . . ."*

Elizabeth switched off the ignition and threw the door open. Play was already resuming. How was she going to get to Jeffrey now? "Come on!" she yelled to Ronnie.

Together they ran past the bleachers directly to the Cyclone fence that separated the field from the seats, right behind the Gladiators' bench. A few yards in front of Elizabeth, Coach Horner was staring out onto the field, looking worried.

"Coach Horner!" Elizabeth cried out.

The coach reacted angrily to something on the field. He cupped one hand to his mouth and shouted, "Come on, French! Heads up!"

"*Coach Horner!*" Ronnie yelled.

Coach Horner looked around with a start. Giving Elizabeth and Ronnie a blank, dismissive look, he began to turn back to the game.

"I need to talk to you right now!" Elizabeth insisted. "It's something about the game!"

Elizabeth knew that normally the coach would never talk to anyone during a game. But she also knew the coach respected her for her work on *The Oracle* and that he knew she would never do something like this unless it was vitally important. She hoped he would listen to her.

With an impatient look, Coach Horner took a step toward them, keeping one eye on the field. "Make it quick, OK?"

"You have to call a time-out, Coach," Elizabeth said. "It would take me too long to explain why."

In a gruff, angry voice, Coach Horner said, "I can't just call a time-out for no reas—"

A huge cheer erupted from the other side of the stadium. Coach Horner, Elizabeth, and Ronnie all looked out to see a Big Mesa defender stealing the ball from Jeffrey.

"Aw, no!" Coach Horner groaned, slamming his fist on the fence. "What's gotten into him?"

"That's exactly why you need a time-out!" Elizabeth pleaded. "He's not himself. I have to talk to him!"

Coach Horner looked startled. He stared at Elizabeth sharply, then turned back to the field, where the Sweet Valley goalie was blocking shot after shot by the Big Mesa team.

Without looking back at Elizabeth, Coach Horner walked away from the fence.

Elizabeth's heart sank. *He doesn't believe me,* she thought. She gazed out at Jeffrey and felt a lump in her throat. Even though he appeared to be playing as hard as always, Elizabeth could see the difference in his eyes. He looked so confused and unfocused.

Suddenly a loud whistle pierced the air, and Elizabeth saw a referee running up to the center field. Standing on the sideline, his hands raised in a T shape, was Coach Horner. "Time-out!" he shouted.

Elizabeth's face broke into a grin as Jeffrey jogged off the field. Coach Horner put an arm around him and gestured toward the fence.

Jeffrey's eyes grew wide when he saw Elizabeth. He ran over, a look of concern and bewilderment on his face. "Elizabeth! Ronnie! Where—"

"Jeffrey, it's going to be all right!" Elizabeth blurted out.

"What?"

"You don't have to worry about Ronnie anymore."

Jeffrey glanced furtively behind him, then turned to face Ronnie. "But Big Al is right there." He gestured to the right with his hand, but Ronnie was already looking in that direction.

"I know," Ronnie said with a broad smile. "And it looks like he just had some visitors."

Elizabeth turned to see Al Remsen rising from his seat, his face red with anger. On either side of him was a policeman, holding him by his arms.

Suddenly a deep voice behind them said, "Are you Ronnie Edwards?"

Ronnie seemed shocked as he turned to see another policeman staring at him.

"Yes," he said.

"We picked up Max Roper, and he gave us your description. We need you to come to the station house for questioning."

Ronnie gulped. "OK." He looked back at Elizabeth and Jeffrey. Underneath his crestfallen expression Elizabeth thought she could see a glimmer of relief.

"Well, I'd better go," Ronnie replied. "Good luck, Jeffrey. I'm sorry for everything."

"Bye, Ronnie," Elizabeth said. As the policeman escorted him away she realized she had lost her anger at him. He had made some bad choices in his life, but it finally looked as if he were facing up to what he'd done.

Jeffrey looked stunned. "What happened?"

Elizabeth smiled. "It's a long story."

"Is Ronnie in trouble?"

"Ronnie's in better shape now than he's been in for weeks. You won't believe how heroically he acted today. But we can talk about it during the victory celebrations," Elizabeth told Jeffrey.

"Right," Jeffrey said, his eyes regaining their old sparkle. He gave Elizabeth a relieved, euphoric grin. "The victory celebration!"

Just then the buzzer sounded, signaling the end of the time-out.

With a whoop of joy, Jeffrey charged back onto the field.

Fifteen

"Score!" the referee shouted, raising his arms in the air.

Elizabeth jumped out of her seat and yelled as loudly as she could. The Sweet Valley side of the stadium was as wild as the Big Mesa side was silent. The score was 3-2, in favor of the Gladiators, with one minute left, and the last two Sweet Valley goals had been scored by Jeffrey!

On the field, Jeffrey and Aaron exchanged a high five. A few feet away, Jack Everly stood scowling. He had been defending Jeffrey the whole second half of the game, but he might as well have stayed on the bench. Jeffrey was playing the game of his life.

When the final buzzer rang, the roar from the stands sounded like a thunderclap. Then all the Sweet Valley fans swarmed onto the field to celebrate the victory.

Elizabeth ran onto the field and threw her arms around Jeffrey. Laughing, Jeffrey lifted her off the ground and swung her in a circle.

As he set her down gently, she looked up into his eyes. She wanted so much to see the spark that had been missing this past week.

Jeffrey smiled back at her as if he could read her mind. Then his lips met hers in a long kiss that made the crowded stadium disappear for a minute or two.

As Elizabeth and Jeffrey walked through the parking lot toward the Fiat after he had taken a shower and had his picture taken for the *Sweet Valley News*, she explained what had happened that afternoon. Jeffrey listened silently, his expression growing more solemn as she described Max's attempt to gag her.

By the time she finished, they were leaning against the car. Jeffrey's arm was wrapped around her, his eyes full of concern. "Are you sure you're OK?" he asked. "Maybe we should drive to the hospital."

"No, I'm fine. But I think it's going to take Ronnie a while to recover."

"Well, I'm more concerned about you," Jeffrey said, running his hands through her hair. "I feel so bad about getting you mixed up in this."

Elizabeth let her head roll back and forth with each stroke of his hand. "Mmmm, keep doing that and I'll forgive anything." Just then Elizabeth remembered a question she had been dying to ask. "Jeffrey, you haven't mentioned anything about the scout from Branford."

"Liz, your story is ten times more important! Who cares about the scout?"

"I do." Elizabeth smiled tentatively. She hoped it wasn't the wrong thing to bring up.

Jeffrey's face clouded over. "Well, he did mention something about me to Coach Horner."

Uh-oh, Elizabeth thought. "What did he say?"

Jeffrey looked somberly at Elizabeth. Then he broke into a grin. "He said that if I didn't go to Branford, I'd be making the biggest mistake of my life."

Elizabeth put her hands on her hips. "Jeffrey French, you scared me!" Then she threw her arms around him. "I'm so proud of you!"

"Wait," Jeffrey said, laughing. "There's more. Mr. Russo was in that big crowd on the field. I saw him on the way back to the locker room. He told me he graded the exams last night."

"And . . ." Elizabeth prompted him.

"And . . . guess who's going to stay on the soccer team next year?"

"You're kidding!"

Jeffrey beamed. "B minus."

"Jeffrey, that's fantastic!" Elizabeth gave him a big hug.

"OK, you two, cut it out. This is a public place!"

Elizabeth whirled around at the sound of Jessica's voice. She and A.J. were walking arm in arm toward them. "Where were you, Liz?" Jessica continued. "I didn't get to the game until almost halftime, and you still hadn't shown up!"

"Halftime?" Elizabeth said with amazement. "You were working on your jewelry that long?"

"Well . . ." Jessica said. "I had to go to see Ms. Lussier."

"Oh?"

Jessica shrugged. "It turns out the Wakefield line will just have to make its debut at another store."

"What happened?"

"Treasure Island is becoming a clothing store, and they're cutting back on jewelry. I tried to convince Ms. Lussier to keep my line, but she wouldn't do it," Jessica explained.

"Can you sell your pieces anywhere else?"

"All fifty of them?" Jessica sighed. "I would have to work eight hours a day, send samples to dozens of stores . . ."

Elizabeth could tell from her sister's tone of voice that jewelry-making was about to go the way of her other unsuccessful money-making projects.

A.J. took Jessica's hand. "Listen, guys, we'll see you at the Dairi Burger, OK?" he said.

"Sure. See you there." Elizabeth made a mental note to find some private time with her sister at the Dairi Burger later on. She felt as if she hadn't seen her at all in the past week. Elizabeth and Jeffrey climbed into her car to head for their favorite hangout, but as she put the key in the ignition, Jeffrey gripped her hand.

"I have a promise to make," he said. "From now on, no more secrets. I feel so bad about all of this. I should have talked to you from the beginning."

"I know," Elizabeth said with an impish glint in her eyes. "But you can still try to make it up to me."

Jeffrey leaned closer. "I guess I've got my work cut out for me," he said.

As their lips met, Elizabeth closed her eyes. She had wanted everything to be the way it was between them. But somehow, hard as it was to imagine, things were even better.

The Dairi Burger would just have to wait.

Sixteen

"Nine hundred dollars?" Mr. Wakefield glared at Jessica. In his right hand he clutched a credit-card bill. "You charged nine hundred dollars? For what?"

Jessica felt like crawling under the rug and hiding. It took a lot to get her father angry, and today she had definitely succeeded.

She knew she should have told her parents about the money earlier, but she hadn't had time to build up the courage. It was less than two weeks ago that she had bought the jewelry materials. Who would have thought the bill would come so fast? Didn't they have to process it or something? she wondered. She had been counting on that extra time.

"Jewelry materials, Dad," Jessica said meekly. "I thought I'd make a bigger profit if I sold more—"

"No wonder the gas station wouldn't let me use that card," Ned Wakefield interrupted, throwing his hands in the air. "We're over our credit limit!" He shook his head. "And there I was trying to convince them *they* had made a mistake."

"We know what your reasons were, Jessica," Mrs. Wakefield said. "But the point is, you said you were going to charge five hundred at the most. Even that seemed like too much."

"I know, Mom," Jessica answered, "but the salesman was quoting me all these great prices, and I kept thinking of what Ms. Lussier promised me. I mean, she *said* she'd take as many as I could make."

"Yes, but you must have made fifty pieces for her—and you've got half the material left over! And what if she *had* taken your jewelry and then found out it wasn't selling anyway?"

"Well, I was trying to think positive, Mom. Like you always say we should."

"All right," Mrs. Wakefield said. "You got yourself into this jam, and you're going to have to figure a positive way out. Your father and I won't be able to use this card until some of your charges are paid back. The bills are going to come in every month, and even if you just pay the minimum, Jess, it's still going to be a lot."

Jessica's face brightened. "Oh, I know. I'm

going to take my pieces around to other stores. Treasure Island isn't the *only* place in Sweet Valley that sells jewelry."

"Just a minute," Mr. Wakefield said. "Maybe you ought to think of something a little more secure, at least until the bill is paid. Selling the jewelry is a chancy thing. First of all, it'll take you a while to get around to all the stores. Second, you don't even know if any stores will take your samples, and the ones that do may only take one or two. Then they have to sell the samples and *then* decide if they want more."

"Well, I could always get a job as a salesperson at Treasure Island," Jessica said jokingly. "There's been a Help Wanted sign in the window for weeks."

"I think that's a great idea, Jessica," Mr. Wakefield said.

Jessica felt her mouth drop open in shock. She hadn't been serious about her suggestion! After all, she had almost become one of Treasure Island's hottest new designers. It would be too humiliating to work there as a *salesgirl*! "Mom, Dad—I just *couldn't*! Not after what's happened!"

"But it would be steady work," Mrs. Wakefield said with a smile. "And I'm *sure* Ms. Lussier is convinced enough of your sales ability to snap you right up. Look at it this way: You'll get a good insider's view on how the clothing business works. And you'll still be able to try to sell your pieces on the side."

"And you'll be able to pay back your bill," her father added. "Bit by bit."

Great! Jessica thought. *Wait until Lila hears about this! It'll be all over school in an hour!*

"Elizabeth, who's R.A.?" John Pfeifer asked, proofreading the "Eyes and Ears" column in the latest issue of *The Oracle*. Since the soccer season had ended, John had fewer assignments and more time to kill in the office.

"Hmmm?" Elizabeth asked absentmindedly, already in the middle of typing next week's column.

"Right here in your column, it says, 'And is that R.A. who seems to be picking up J.M. every day after school?' "

"Jennifer Mitchell and Rick Andover," Elizabeth said.

"Oh," John said softly. "That's what I figured."

"Why, do you know anything else about them?" She glanced up at John, who was frowning.

Before she could ask him what was wrong, Penny Ayala called out from across the room, "What's with the sports page layout?"

"What do you mean? What's wrong?" John Pfeifer asked, walking over to Penny.

149

"There's a big blank space at the end of the piece on Jeffrey French, and there's a gutter running right down the middle of the page!"

"Oh," John said listlessly. "I guess I counted the ad space wrong."

"Well, can you fill it?" Penny asked impatiently. "Maybe if you can rearrange the baseball article, you can pick up some space. Do you have anything else you can throw in there?"

"I'll take care of it, Penny," John told her.

"Are you sure? Because I can try if you don't have time. We need to send it to the printer to—"

"I said I'll take care of it!" John snapped, practically spitting the words out.

Both Elizabeth and Penny looked at him with shock. John had always been so cheerful and mild-mannered. They had never heard him raise his voice like that.

"Sorry, John," Penny said. "I was only trying to help. We're on a tight schedule for this issue."

"I know that. I'm an editor, too, remember?" he shot back. "It's not that big a deal. It'll get done."

With that, he grabbed the page and walked over to his desk.

The office fell silent as Elizabeth and Penny exchanged a baffled glance. Elizabeth wondered if John's sudden bad mood was the result of reading the "Eyes and Ears" column. She knew

John was pretty good friends with Jennifer Mitchell, a sophomore she didn't know very well. Maybe there was more to their relationship than Elizabeth realized.

*What's come over John Pfeifer? Find out in Sweet Valley High #52, **WHITE LIES**.*

YOUR OWN

SLAM BOOK!

If you've read *Slambook Fever*, Sweet Valley High #48, you know that slam books are the rage at Sweet Valley High. Now *you* can have a slam book of your own! Make up your own categories, such as "Biggest Jock" or "Best Looking," and have your friends fill in the rest! There's a four-page calendar, horoscopes and questions most asked by Sweet Valley readers with answers from Elizabeth and Jessica

It's a must for SWEET VALLEY fans!

☐ 05496- FRANCINE PASCAL'S SWEET VALLEY HIGH
SLAM BOOK
Laurie Pascal Wenk $3.95
